BIGFOOT Boy

2

THE UNKINDNESS OF RAVENS

This is a work of fiction and any resemblance of characters to persons living or dead is purely coincidental.

Kids Can Press acknowledges the financial support of the Government of Ontario, through the Ontario Media Development Corporation's Ontario Book Initiative; the Ontario Arts Council; the Canada Council for the Arts; and the Government of Canada, through the CBF, for our publishing activity.

Published in Canada by
Kids Can Press Ltd.
25 Dockside Drive
Toronto, ON M5A 0B5

Published in the U.S. by
Kids Can Press Ltd.
2250 Military Road
Tonawanda, NY 14150

www.kidscanpress.com

Edited by Karen Li and Stacey Roderick
Designed by Rachel Di Salle and Marie Bartholomew

The hardcover edition of this book is smyth sewn casebound.
The paperback edition of this book is limp sewn with a drawn-on cover.
Manufactured in Shen Zhen, Guang Dong, P.R. China, in 4/2013 by Printplus Limited.

CM 13 0 9 8 7 6 5 4 3 2 1
CM PA 13 0 9 8 7 6 5 4 3 2 1

Library and Archives Canada Cataloguing in Publication

Torres, J., 1969 –
The unkindness of ravens / written by J. Torres ; illustrated by Faith Erin Hicks.

(Bigfoot Boy)
ISBN 978-1-55453-713-6 (bound) ISBN 978-1-55453-714-3 (pbk.)

I. Hicks, Faith Erin II. Title. III. Series: Bigfoot Boy

PN6733.T67U65 2013 j741.5'971 C2012-908288-0

Kids Can Press is a Corus™ Entertainment company

BIGFOOT Boy

2

THE UNKINDNESS OF RAVENS

J. Torres and Faith Erin Hicks

Kids Can Press

For Titus, my little bigfoot.
Love, Da

For my brothers, who are now Bigfoot Men — F. E.H.

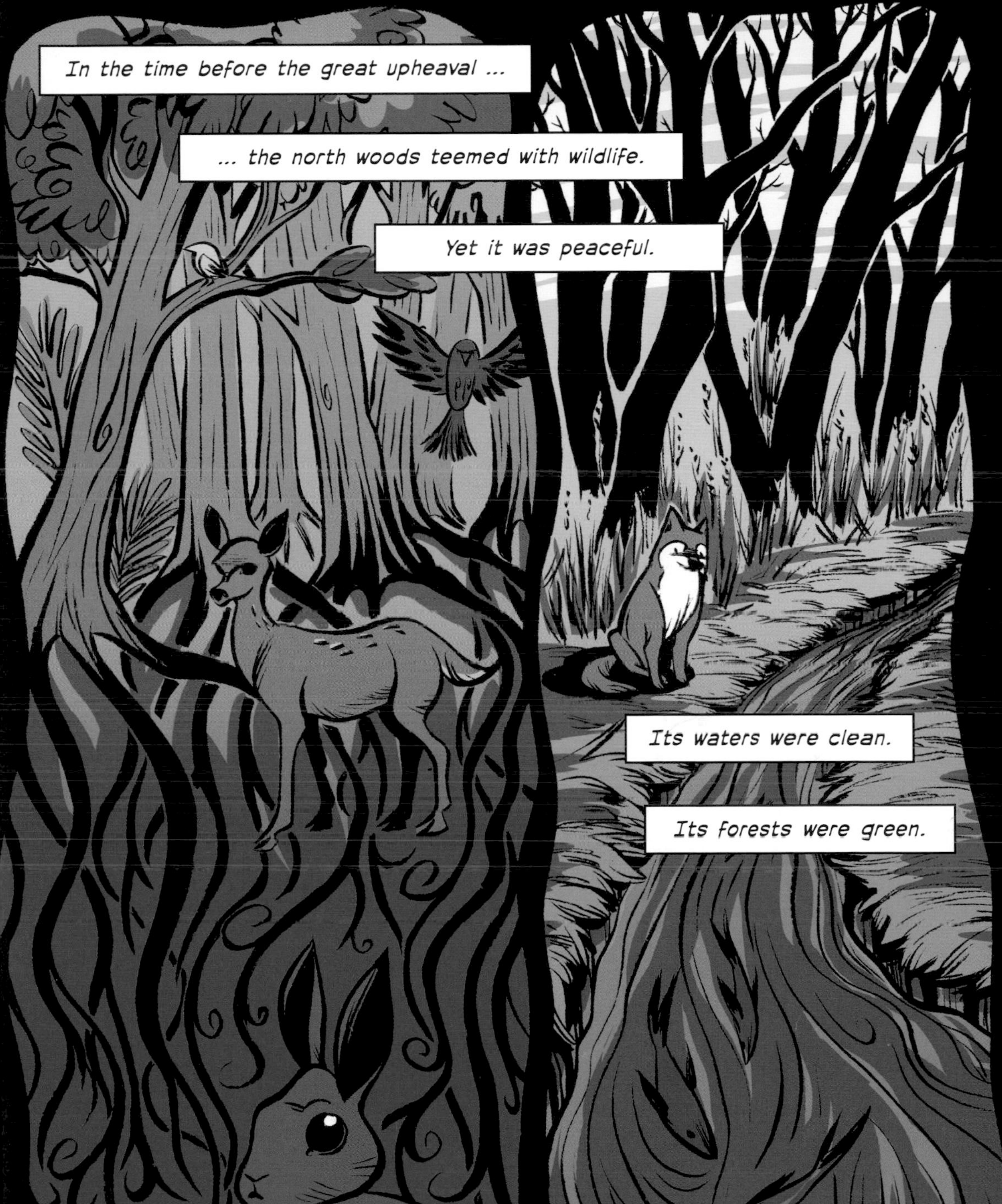
In the time before the great upheaval ...
... the north woods teemed with wildlife.
Yet it was peaceful.
Its waters were clean.
Its forests were green.
The land was whole.

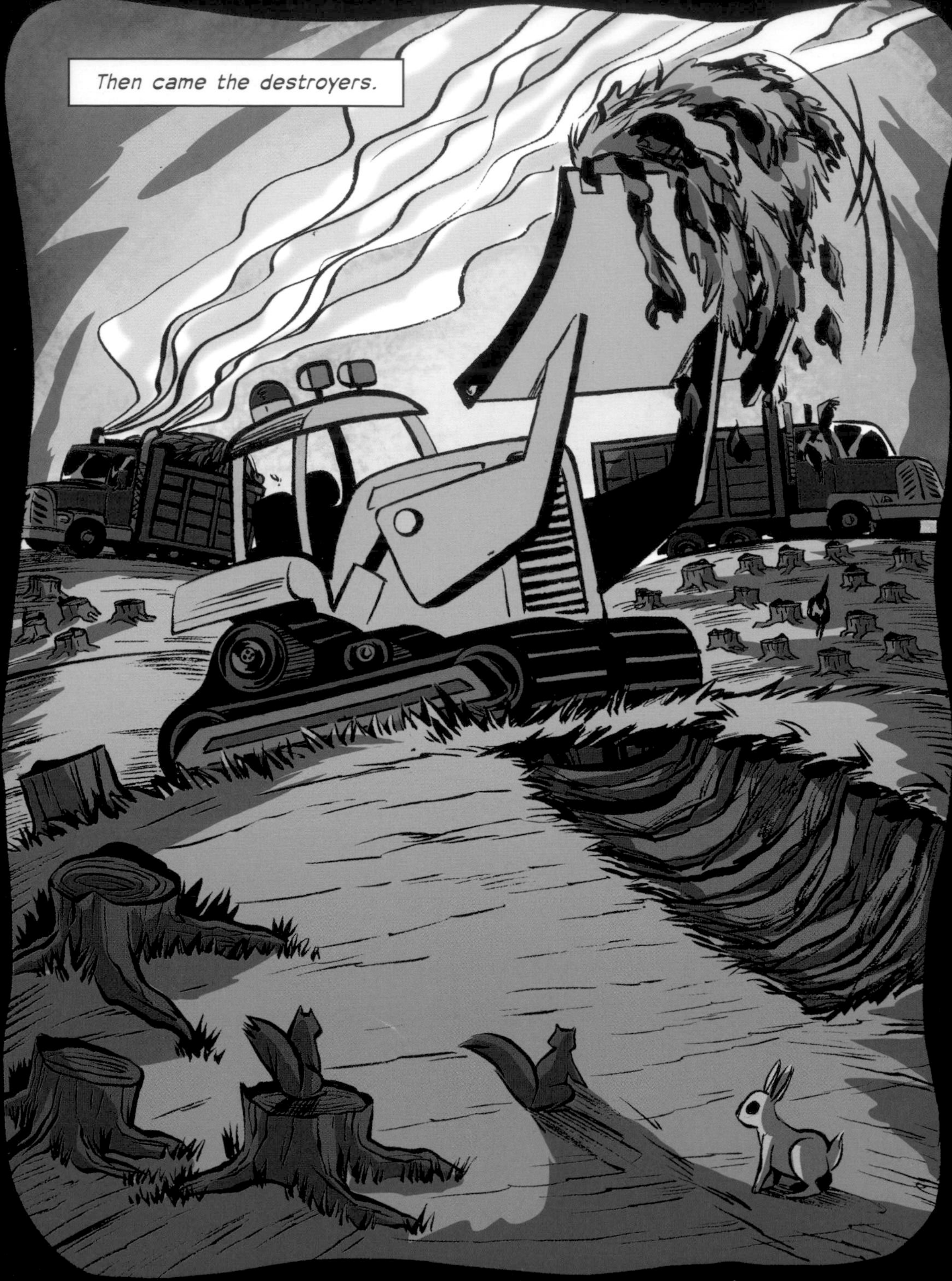
Then came the destroyers.

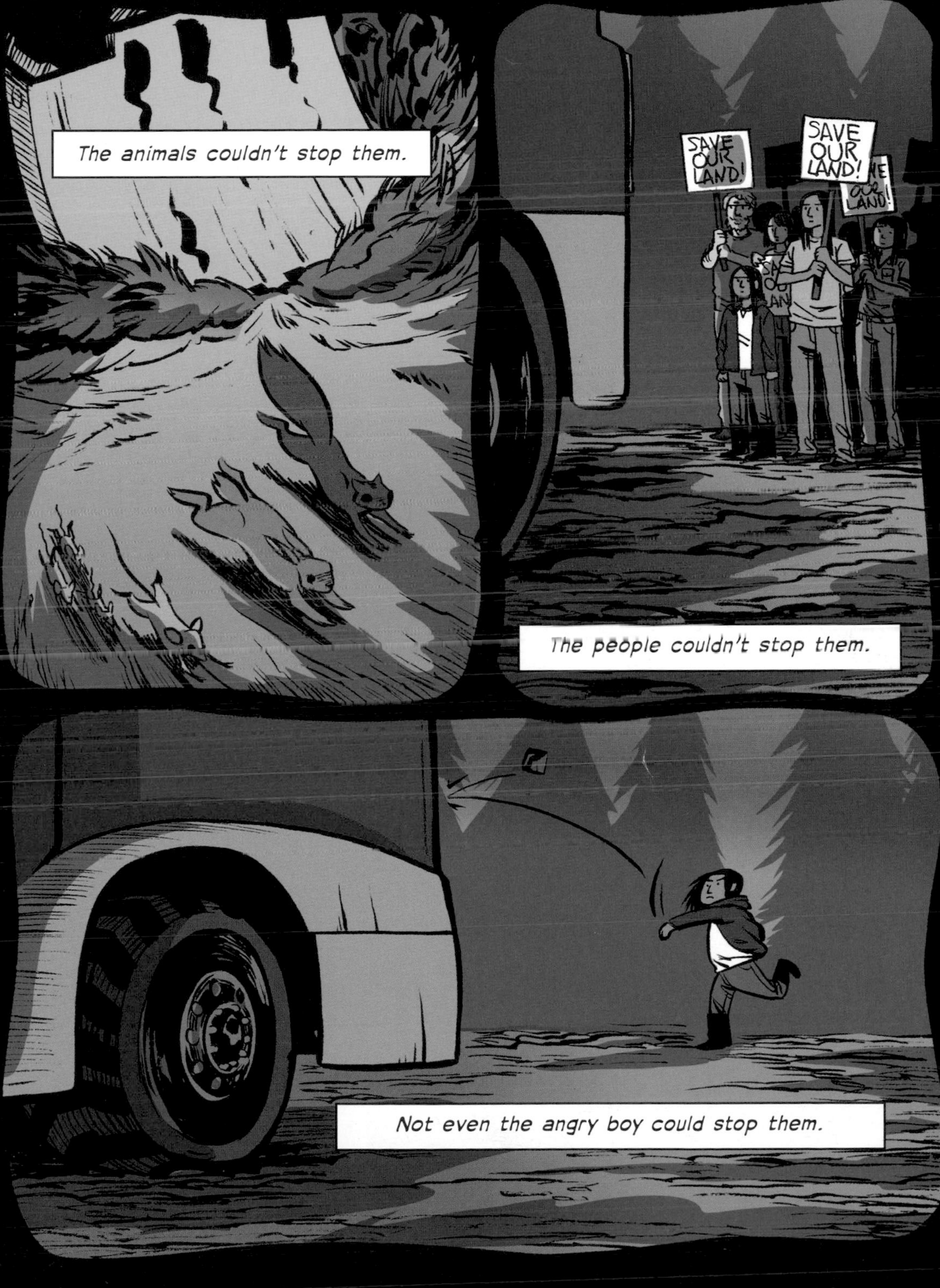
The animals couldn't stop them.
SAVE OUR LAND!
SAVE OUR LAND!
The people couldn't stop them.
Not even the angry boy could stop them.

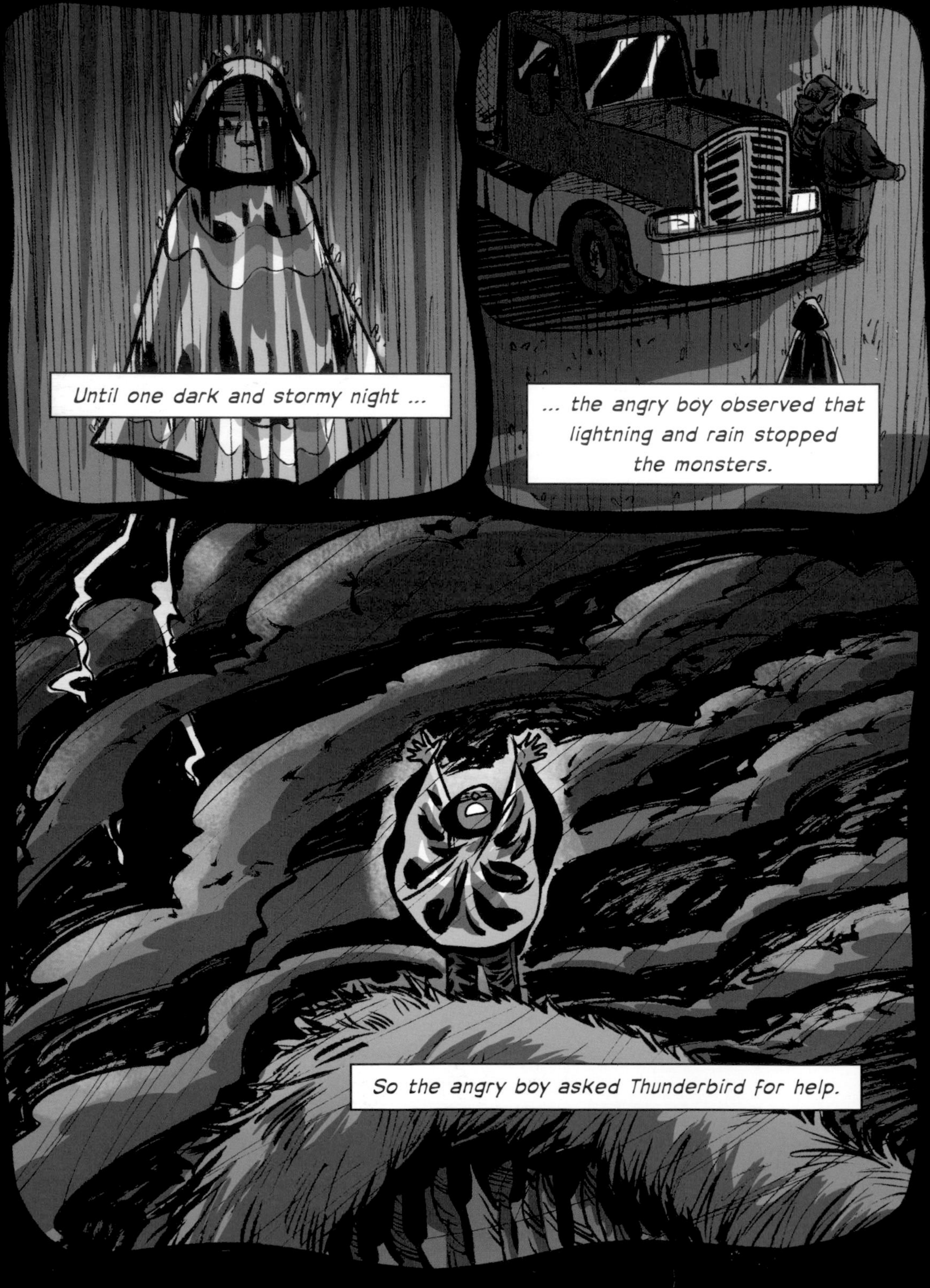
Until one dark and stormy night ...
... the angry boy observed that lightning and rain stopped the monsters.
So the angry boy asked Thunderbird for help.

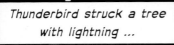

Thunderbird struck a tree with lightning ...

... told the boy to take a branch from that tree ...

... and carve a totem in the form of whatever he saw in his dreams that night.

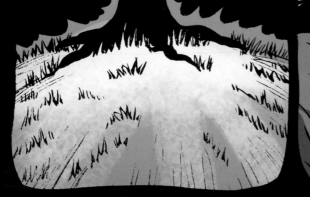

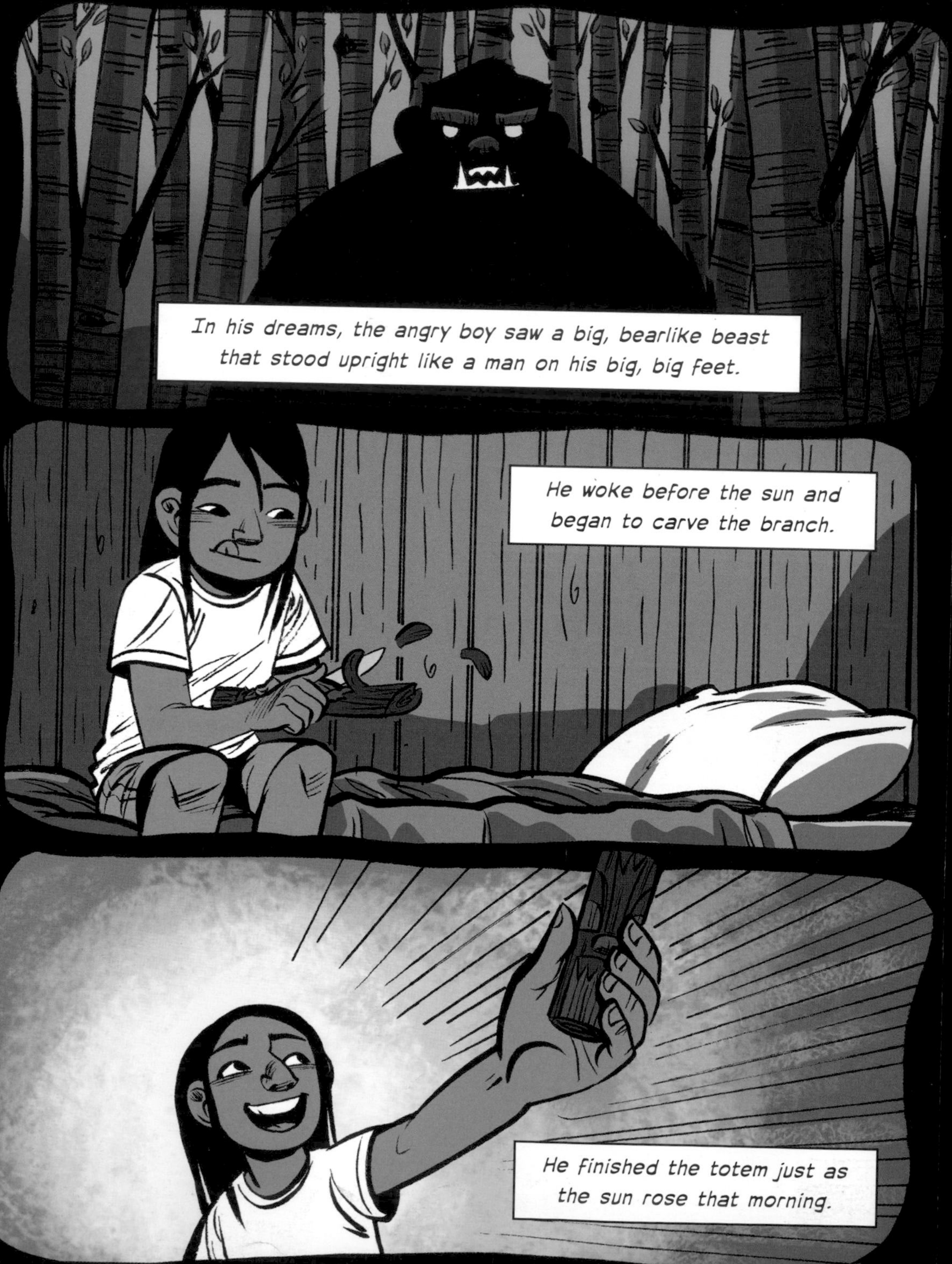
In his dreams, the angry boy saw a big, bearlike beast that stood upright like a man on his big, big feet.
He woke before the sun and began to carve the branch.
He finished the totem just as the sun rose that morning.

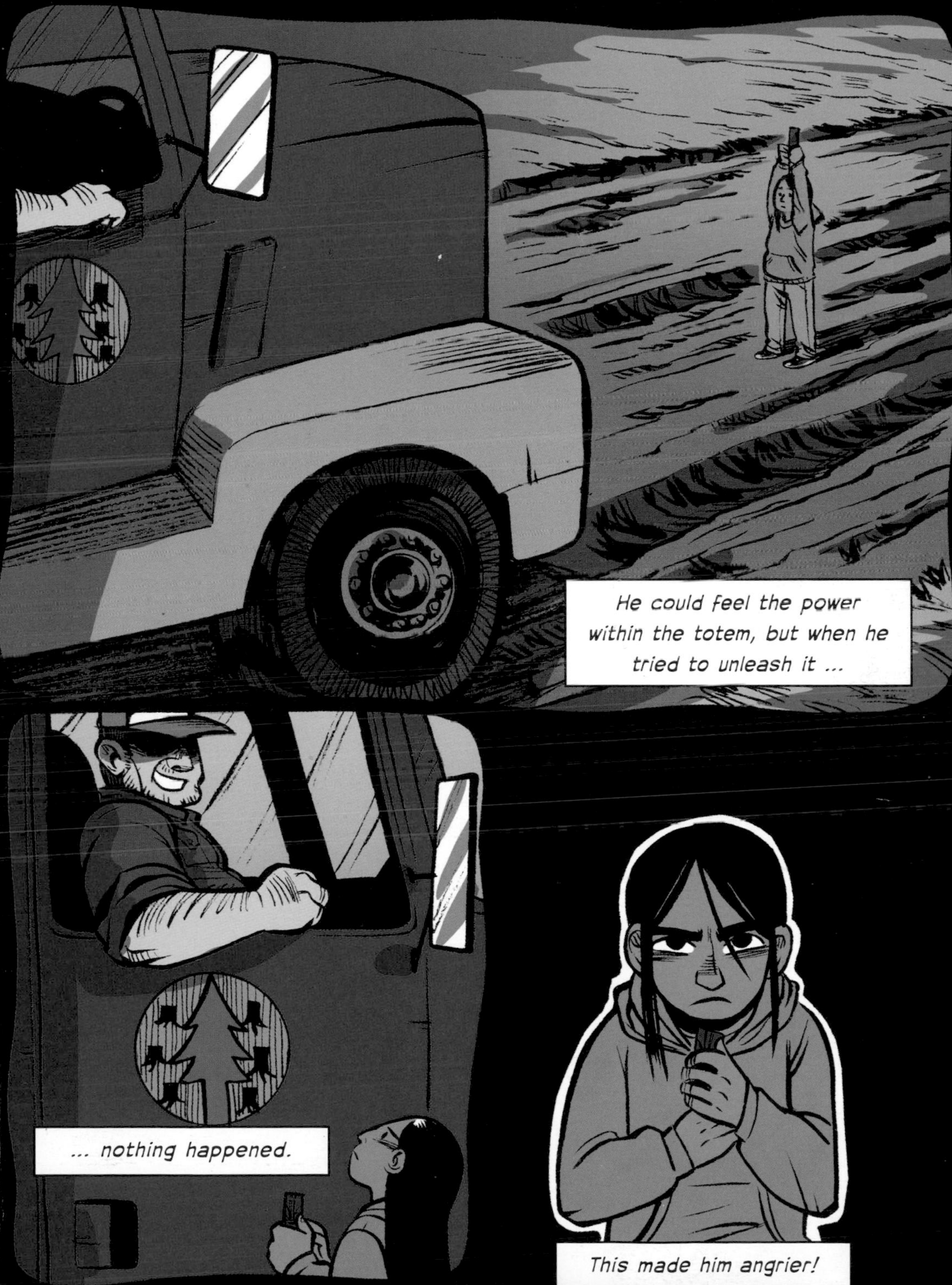
He could feel the power within the totem, but when he tried to unleash it ...
... nothing happened.
This made him angrier!

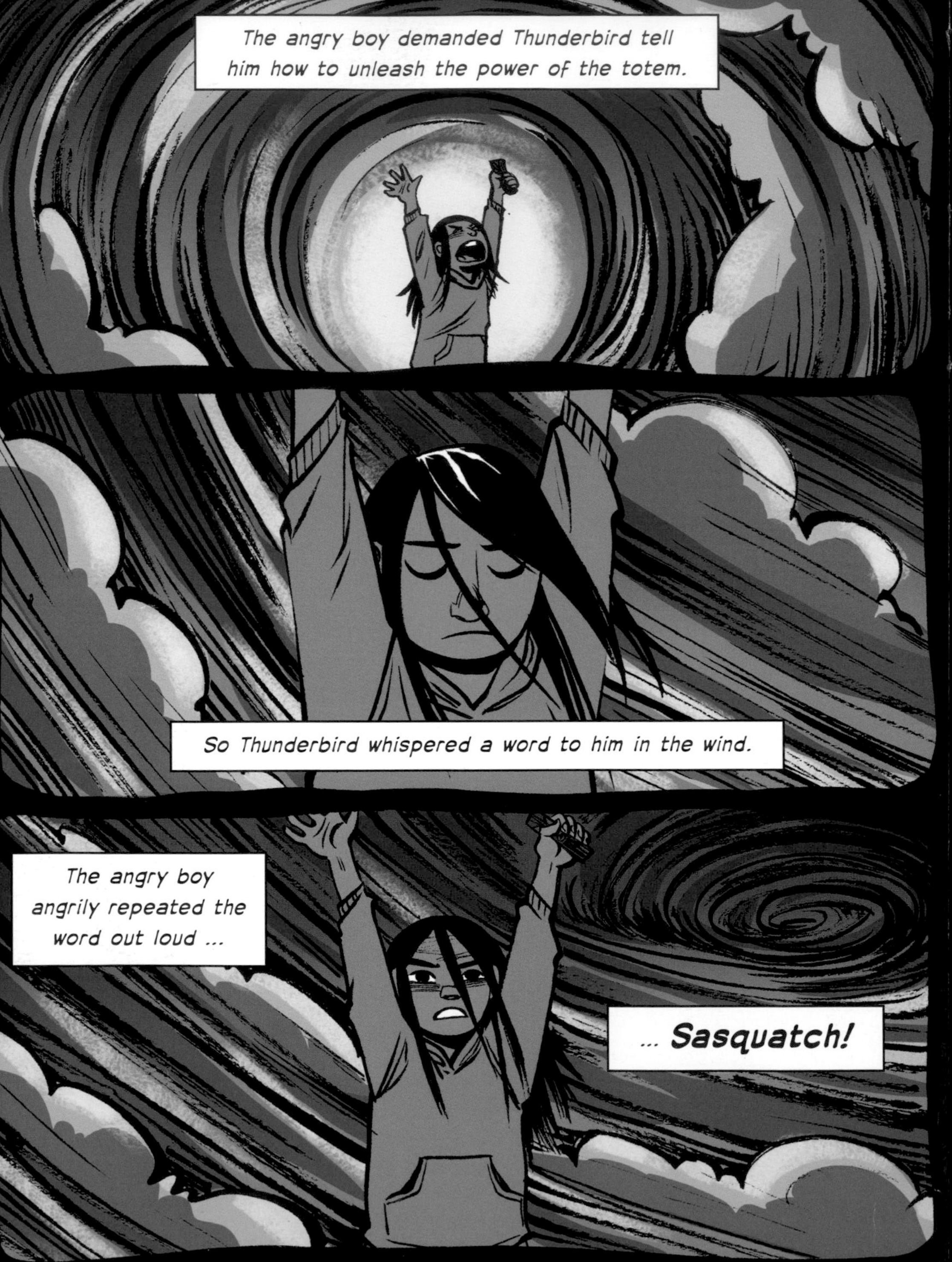
The angry boy demanded Thunderbird tell him how to unleash the power of the totem.
So Thunderbird whispered a word to him in the wind.
The angry boy angrily repeated the word out loud ...
... Sasquatch!

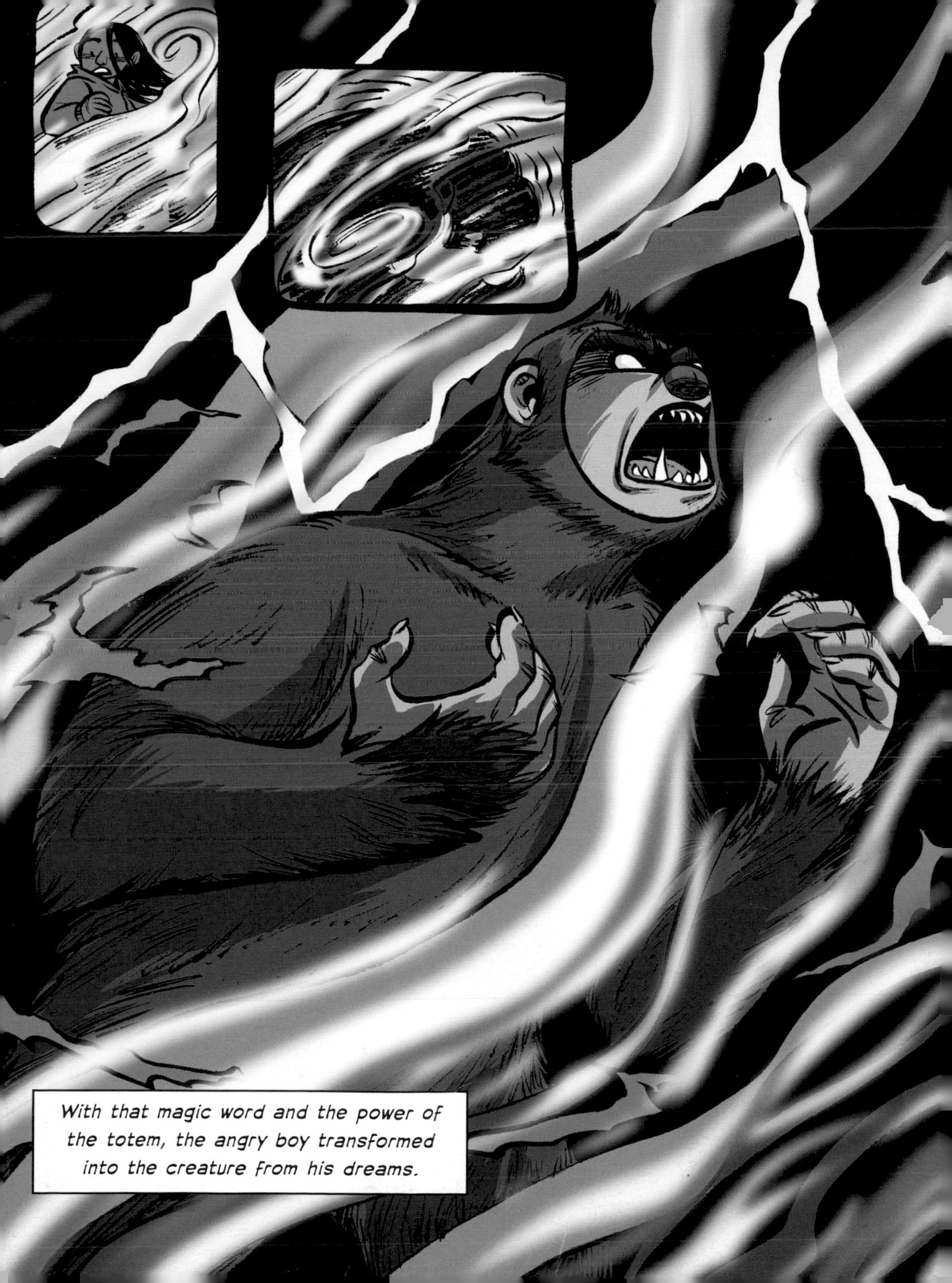
With that magic word and the power of the totem, the angry boy transformed into the creature from his dreams.

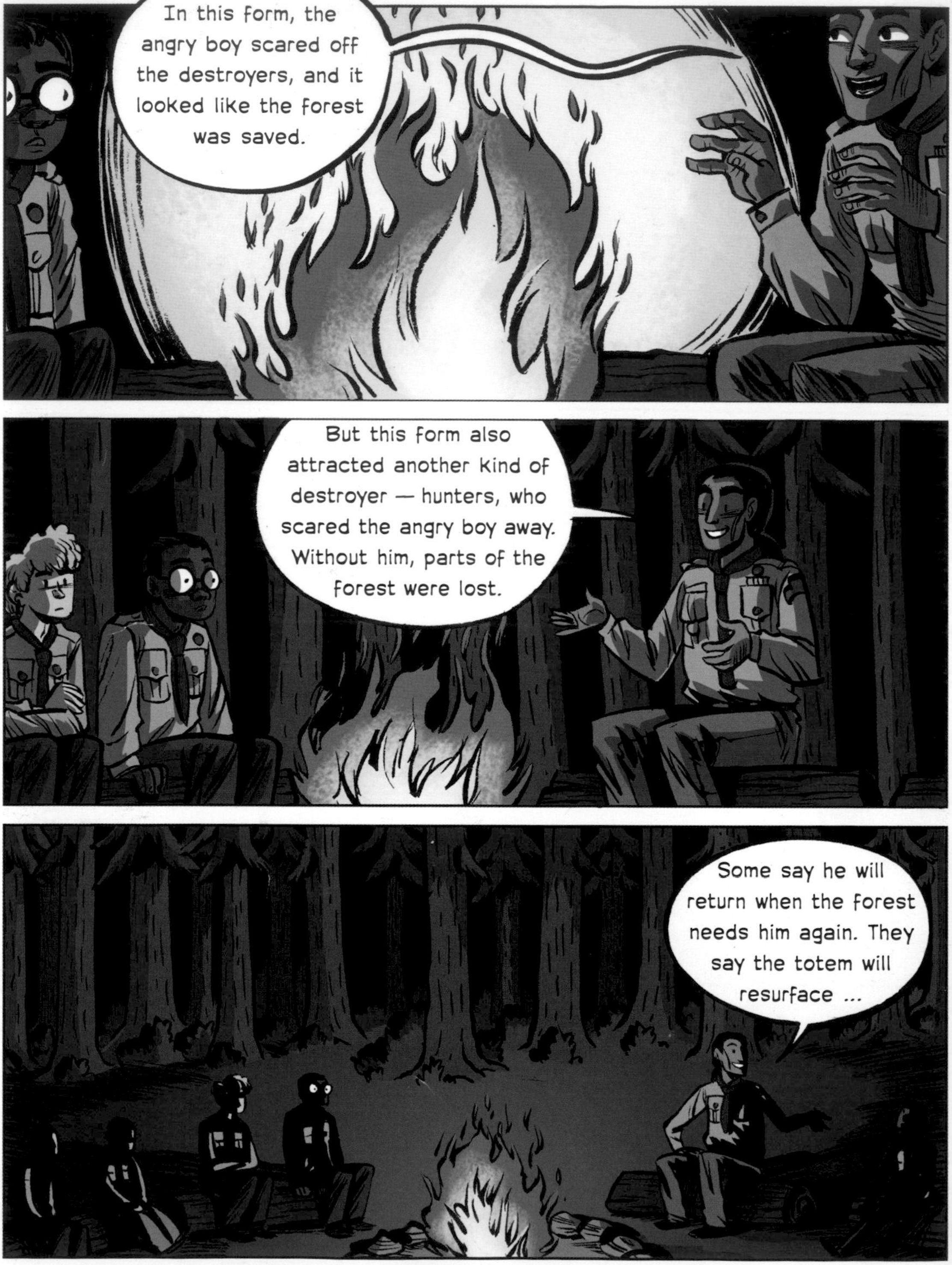
In this form, the angry boy scared off the destroyers, and it looked like the forest was saved.
But this form also attracted another kind of destroyer — hunters, who scared the angry boy away. Without him, parts of the forest were lost.
Some say he will return when the forest needs him again. They say the totem will resurface ...

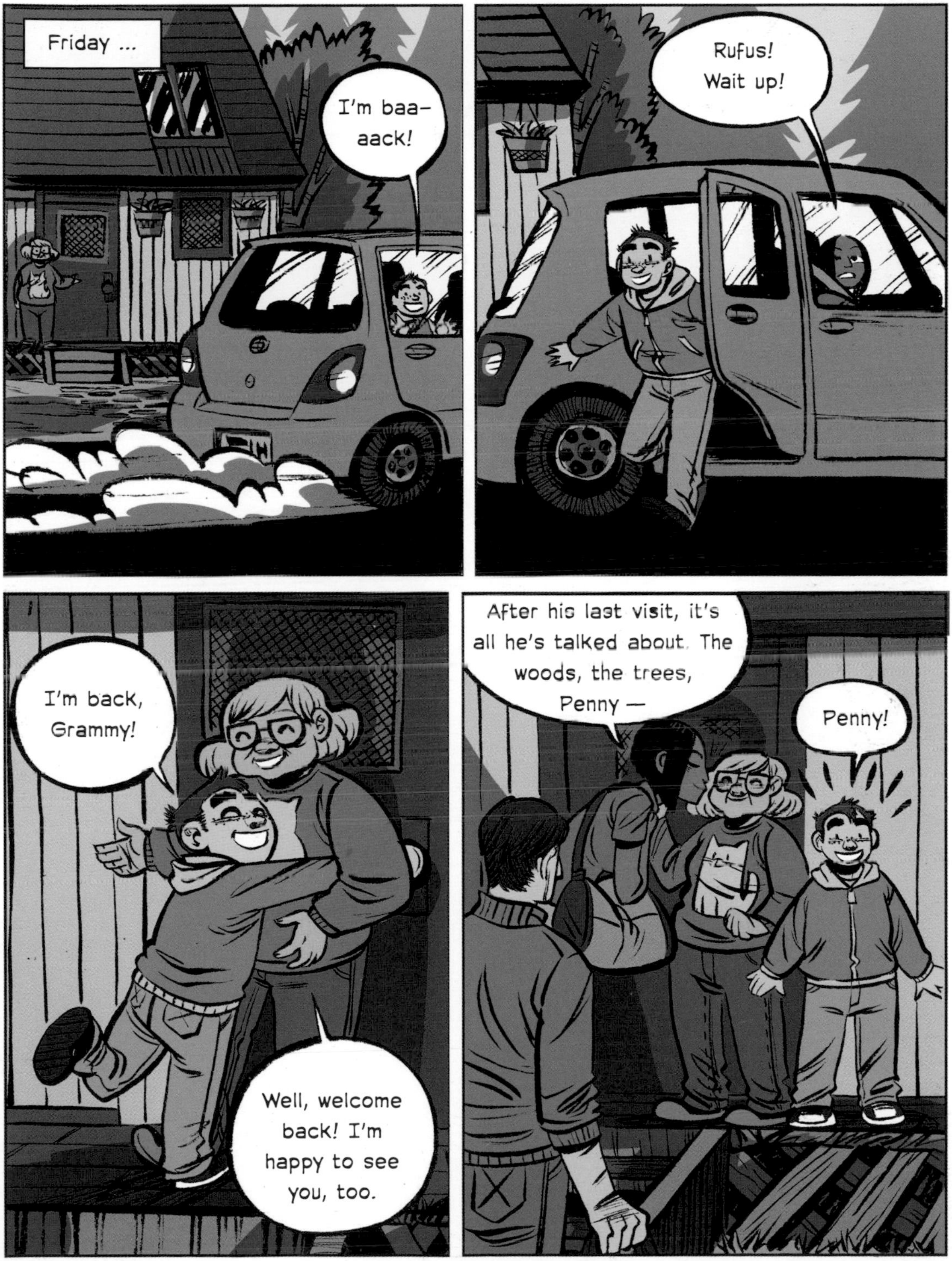
Friday ...
I'm baa-aack!
Rufus! Wait up!
I'm back, Grammy!
Well, welcome back! I'm happy to see you, too.
After his last visit, it's all he's talked about. The woods, the trees, Penny —
Penny!

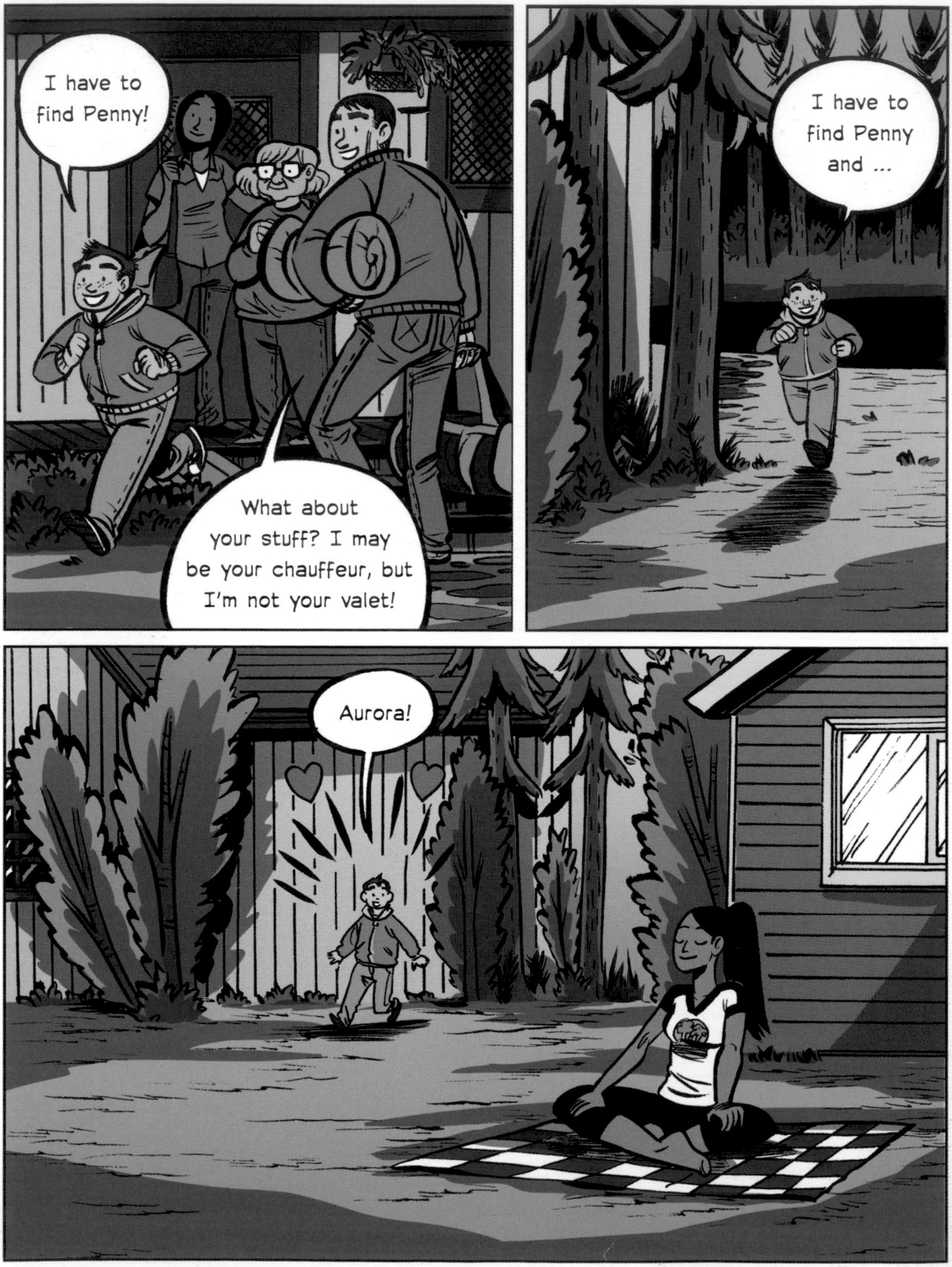
I have to find Penny!
What about your stuff? I may be your chauffeur, but I'm not your valet!
I have to find Penny and ...
Aurora!

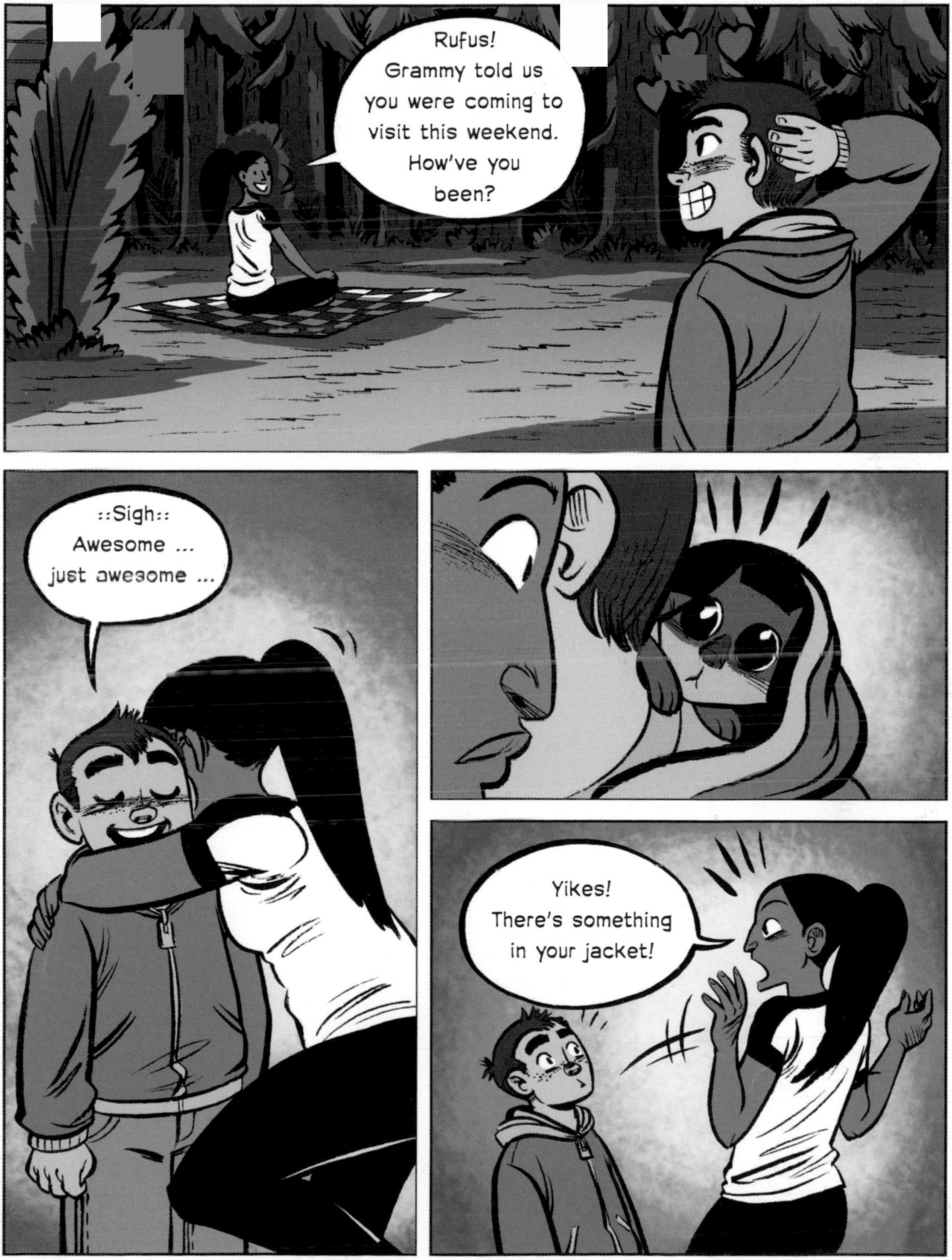
Rufus! Grammy told us you were coming to visit this weekend. How've you been?
::Sigh:: Awesome ... just awesome ...
Yikes! There's something in your jacket!

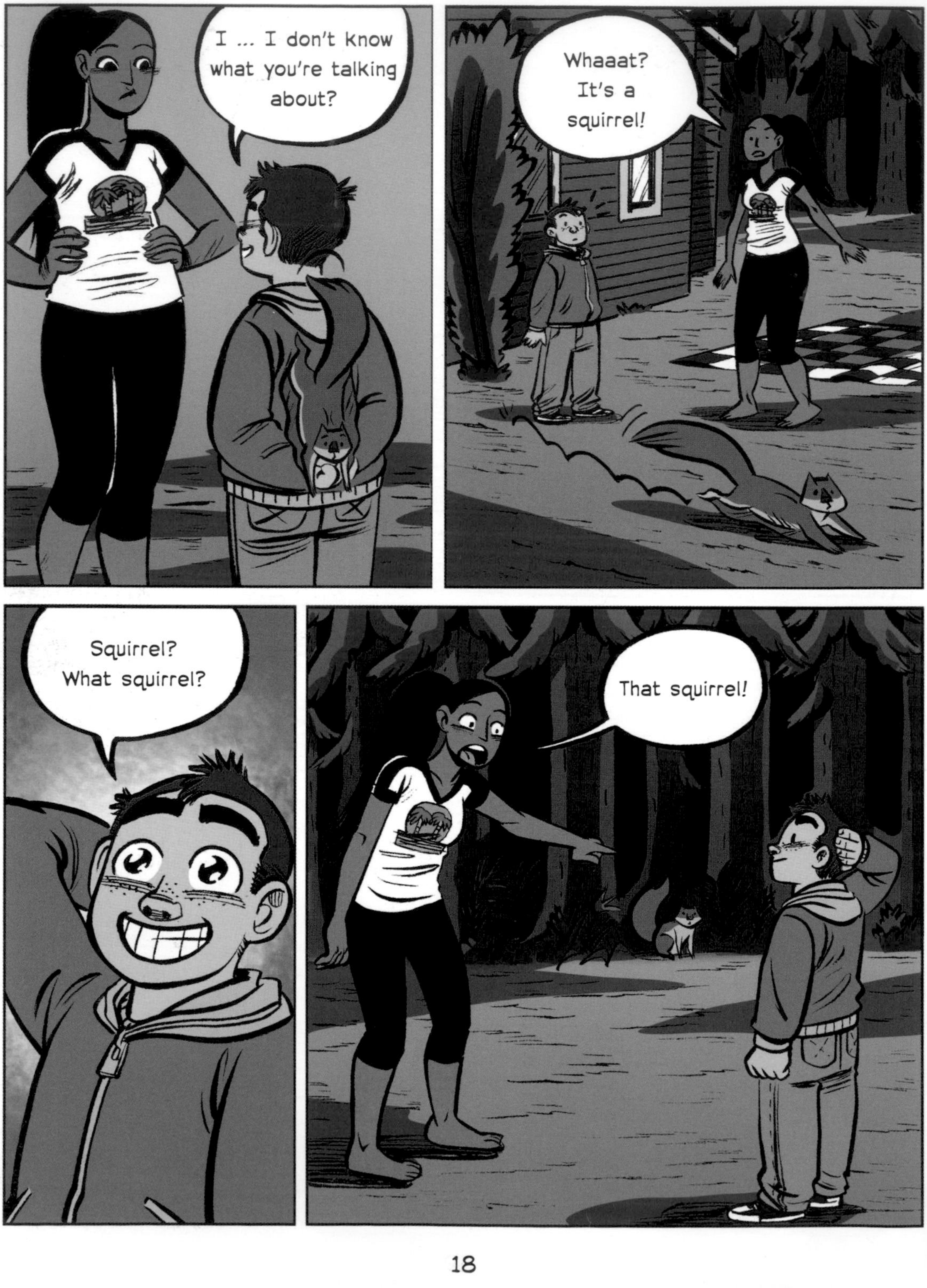
I ... I don't know what you're talking about?
Whaaat? It's a squirrel!
Squirrel? What squirrel?
That squirrel!

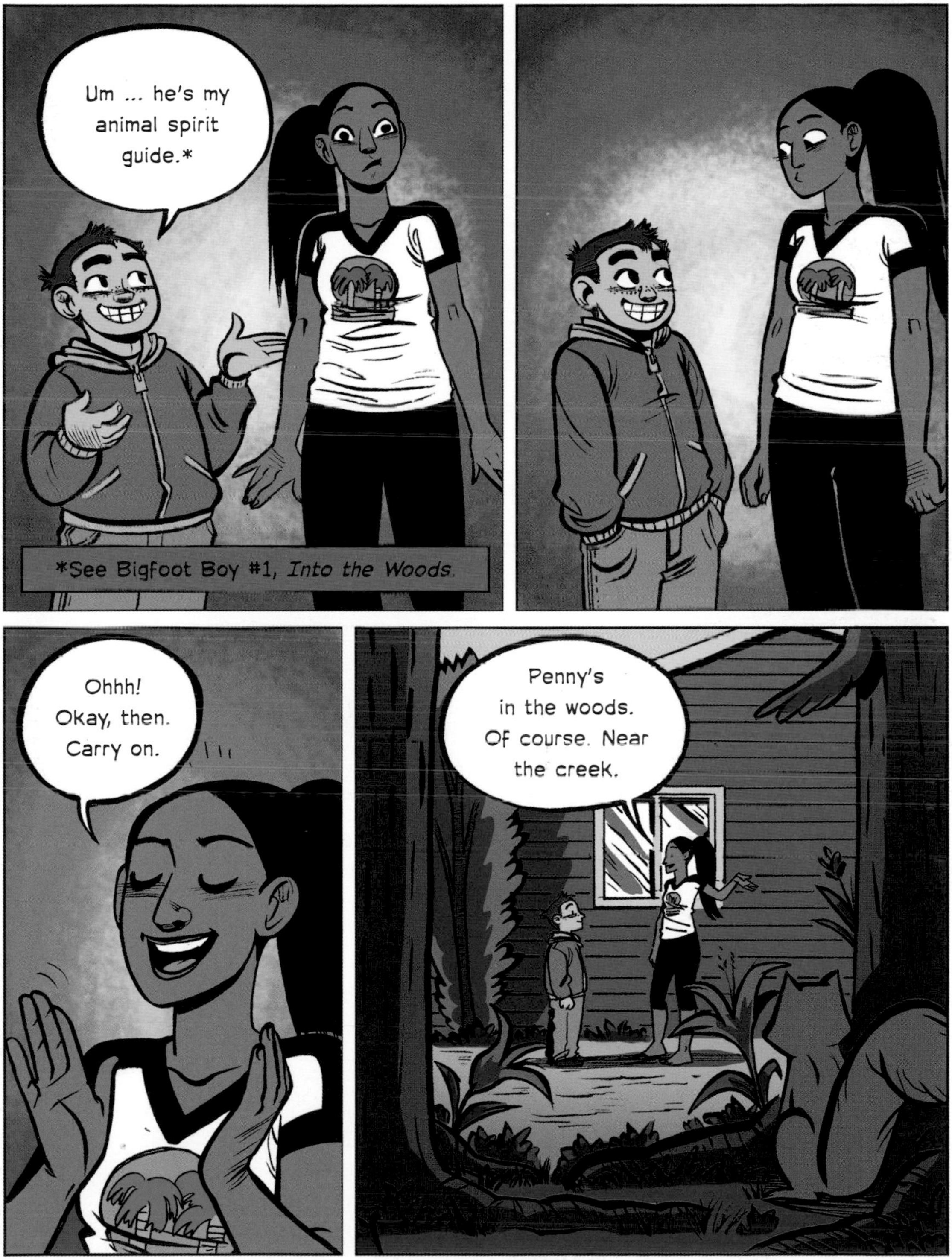
Um ... he's my animal spirit guide.*
*See Bigfoot Boy #1, *Into the Woods.*
Ohhh! Okay, then. Carry on.
Penny's in the woods. Of course. Near the creek.

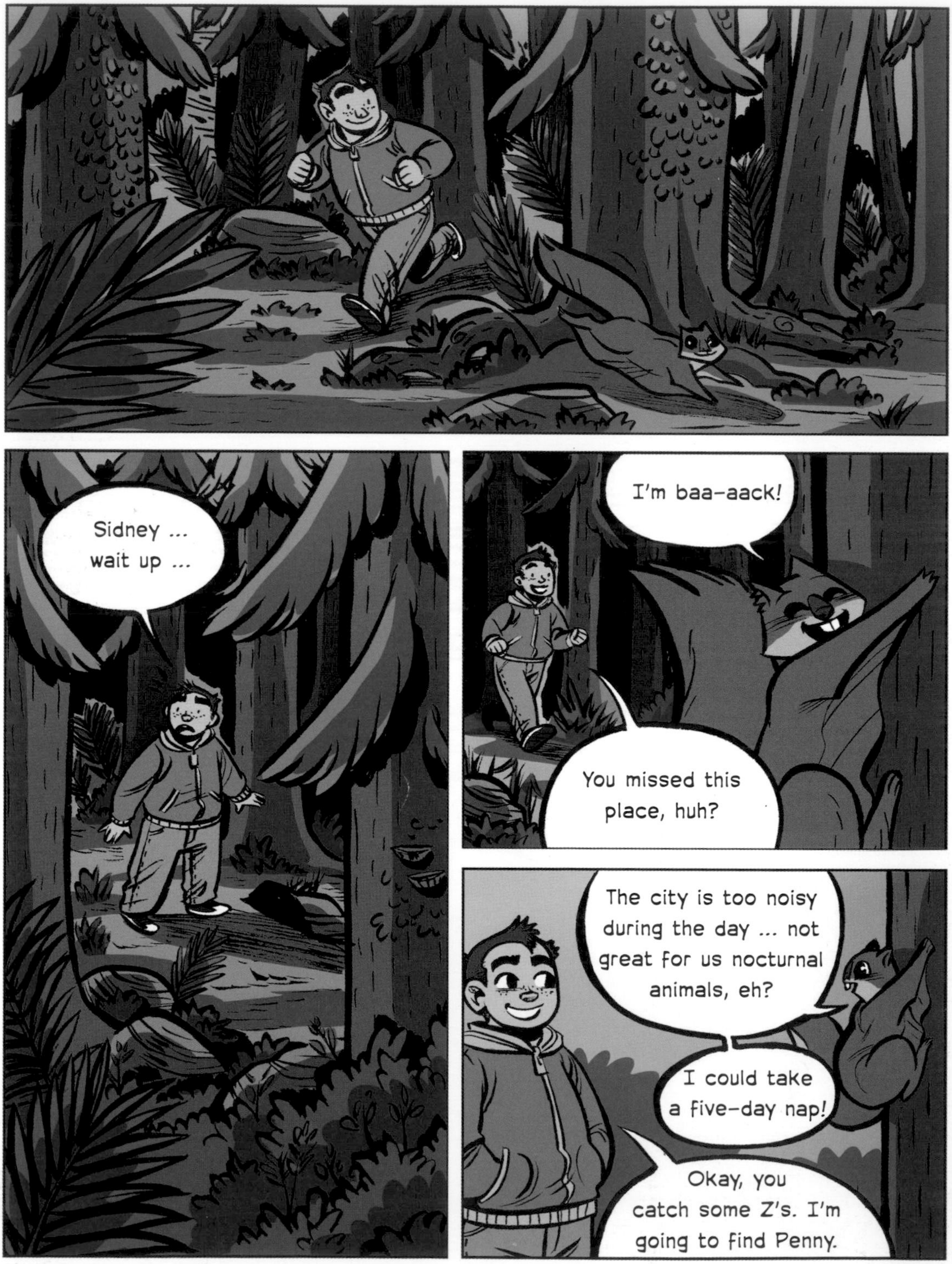
Sidney ... wait up ...
I'm baa-aack!
You missed this place, huh?
The city is too noisy during the day ... not great for us nocturnal animals, eh?
I could take a five-day nap!
Okay, you catch some Z's. I'm going to find Penny.

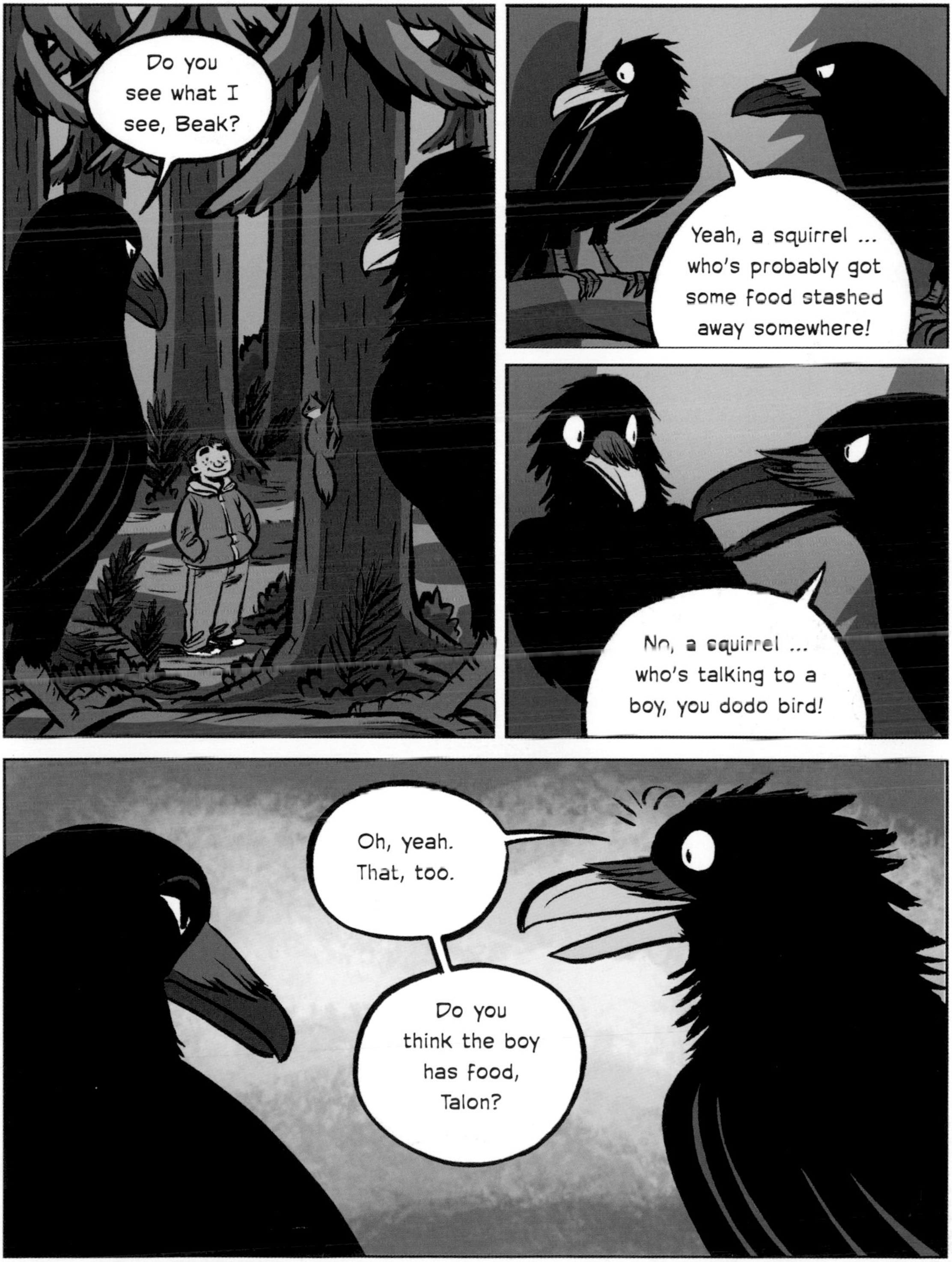
Do you see what I see, Beak?
Yeah, a squirrel ... who's probably got some food stashed away somewhere!
No, a squirrel ... who's talking to a boy, you dodo bird!
Oh, yeah. That, too.
Do you think the boy has food, Talon?

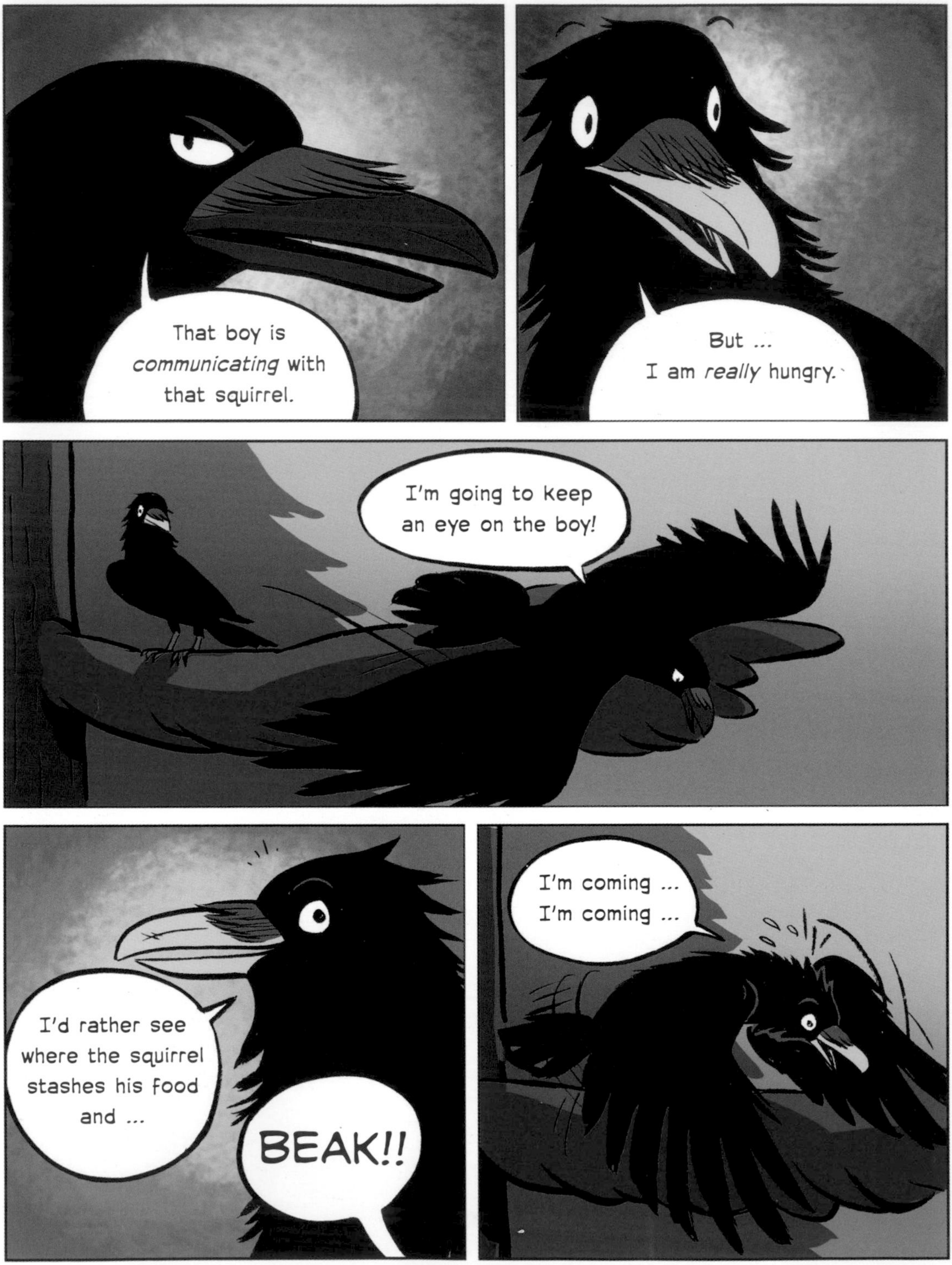
That boy is *communicating* with that squirrel.
But ... I am *really* hungry.
I'm going to keep an eye on the boy!
I'd rather see where the squirrel stashes his food and ...
BEAK!!
I'm coming ... I'm coming ...

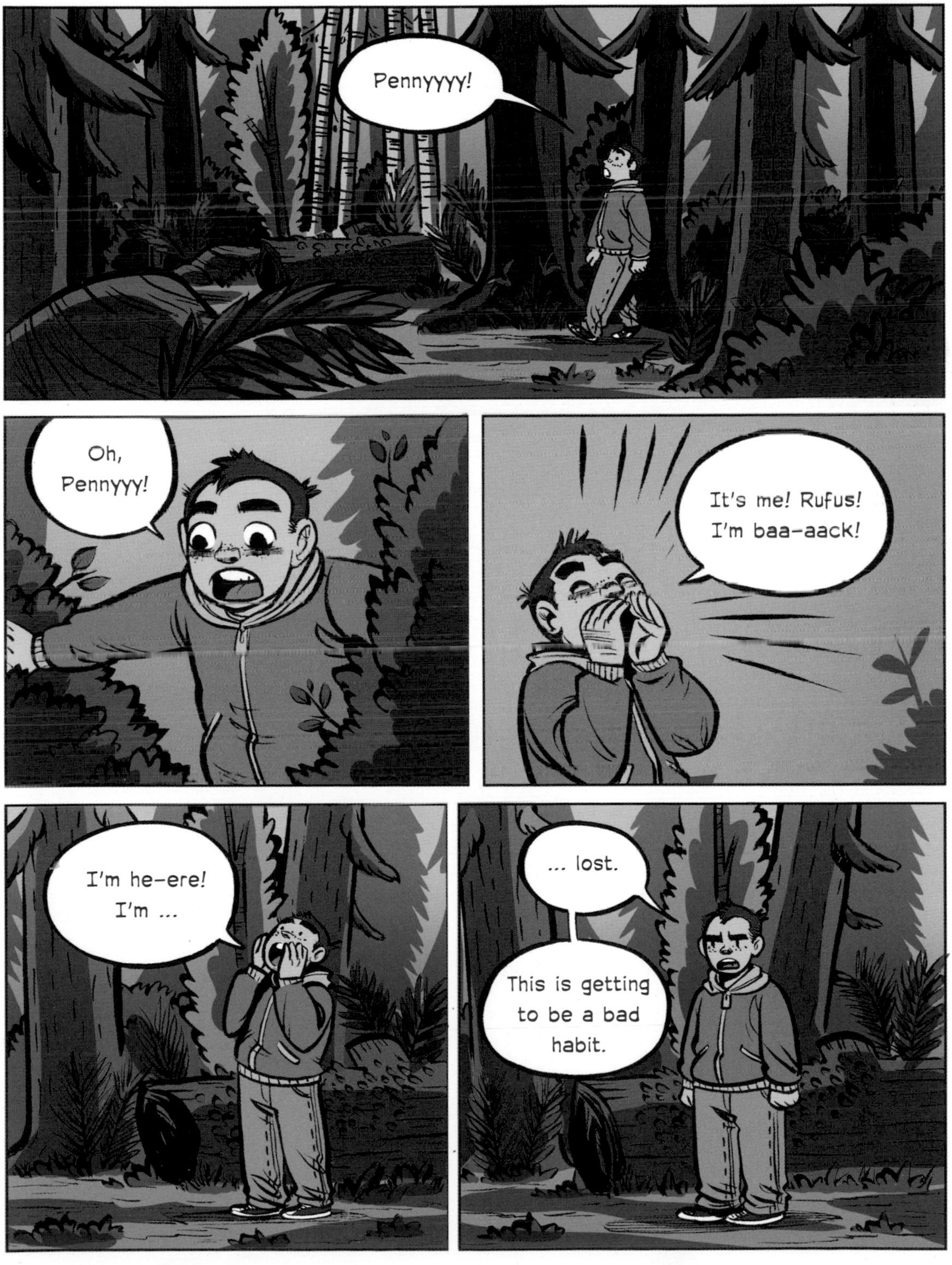
Pennyyyy!
Oh, Pennyyy!
It's me! Rufus! I'm baa-aack!
I'm he-ere! I'm ...
... lost.
This is getting to be a bad habit.

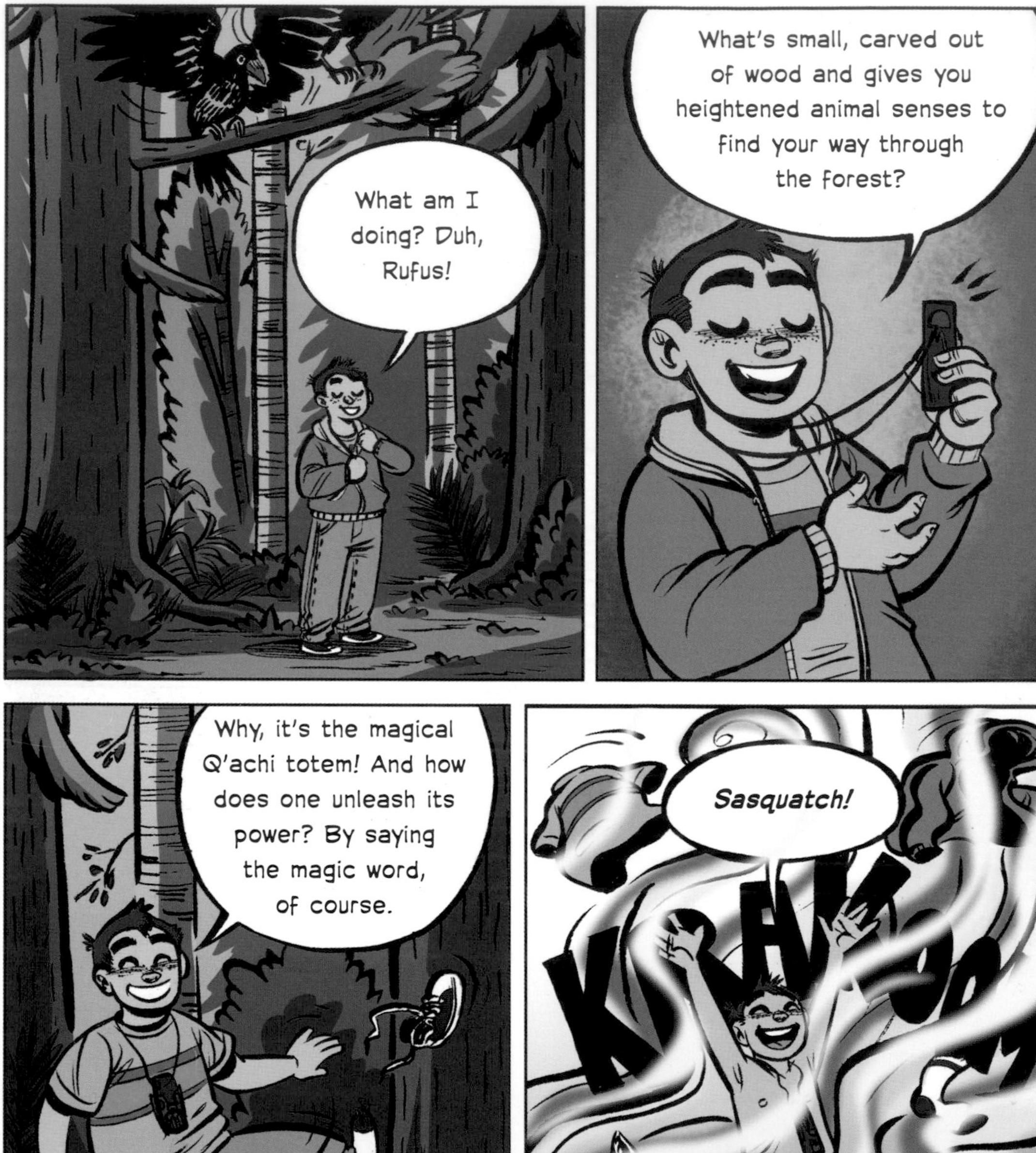
What am I doing? Duh, Rufus!
What's small, carved out of wood and gives you heightened animal senses to find your way through the forest?
Why, it's the magical Q'achi totem! And how does one unleash its power? By saying the magic word, of course.
Sasquatch!

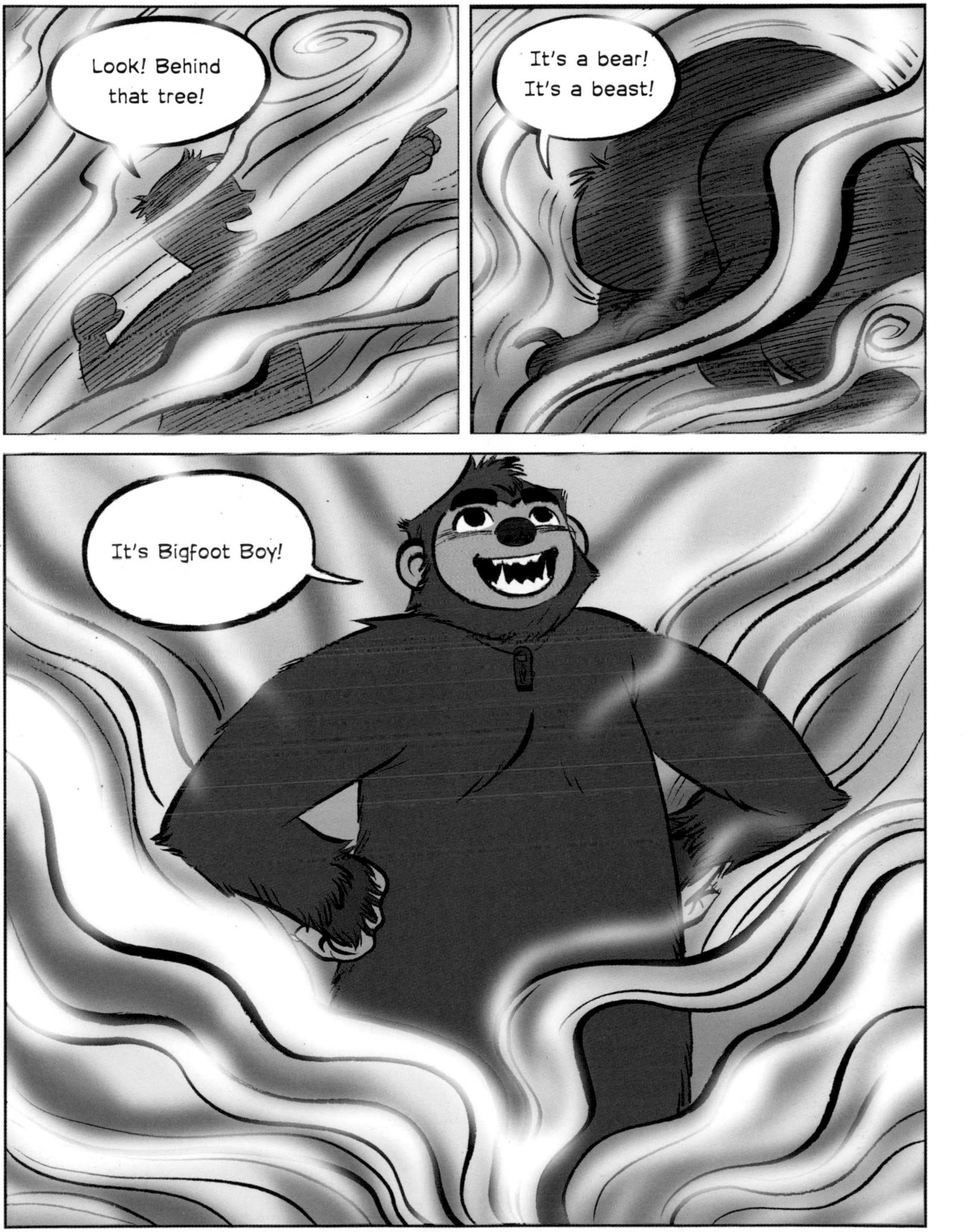
Look! Behind that tree!
It's a bear! It's a beast!
It's Bigfoot Boy!

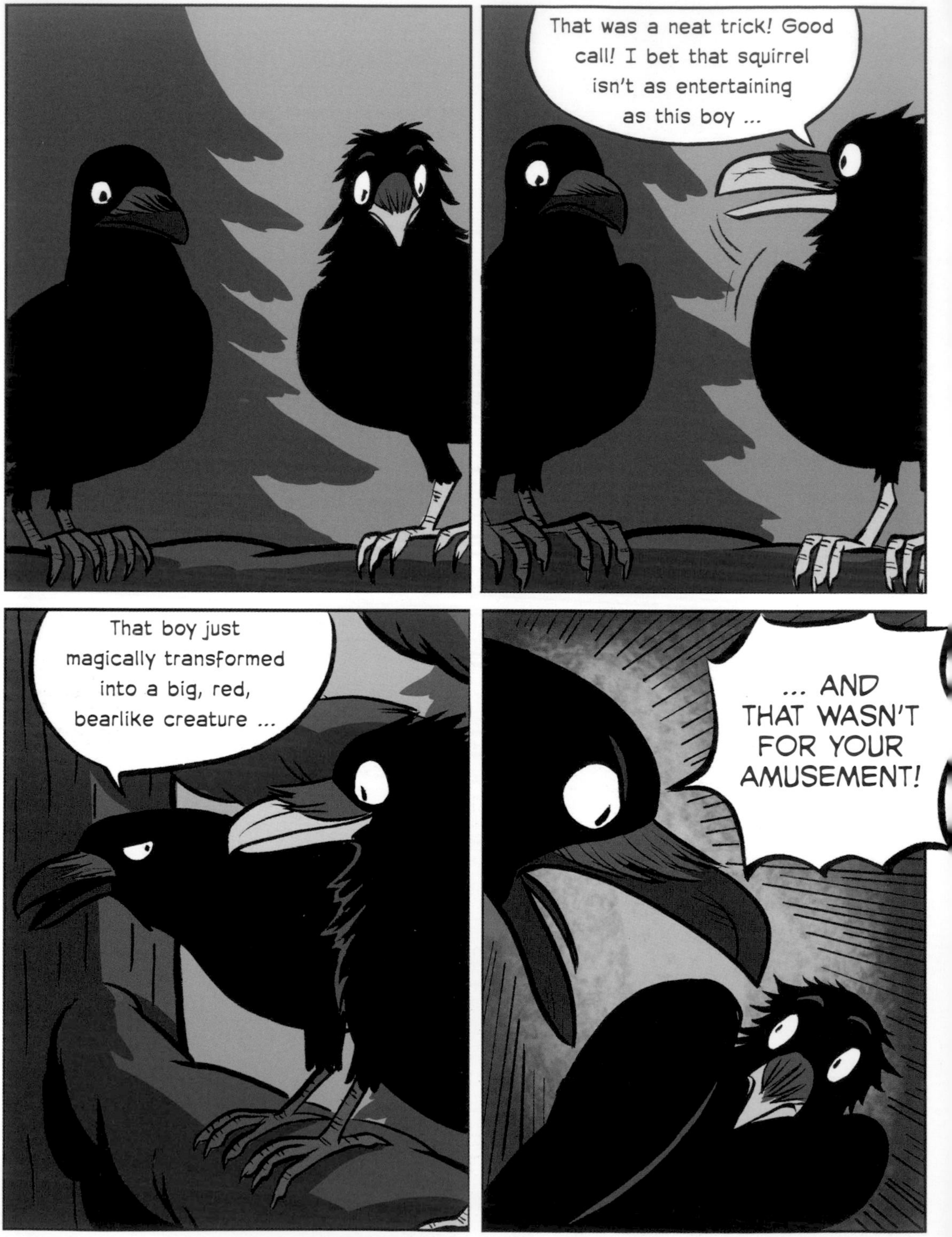
That was a neat trick! Good call! I bet that squirrel isn't as entertaining as this boy ...
That boy just magically transformed into a big, red, bearlike creature ...
... AND THAT WASN'T FOR YOUR AMUSEMENT!

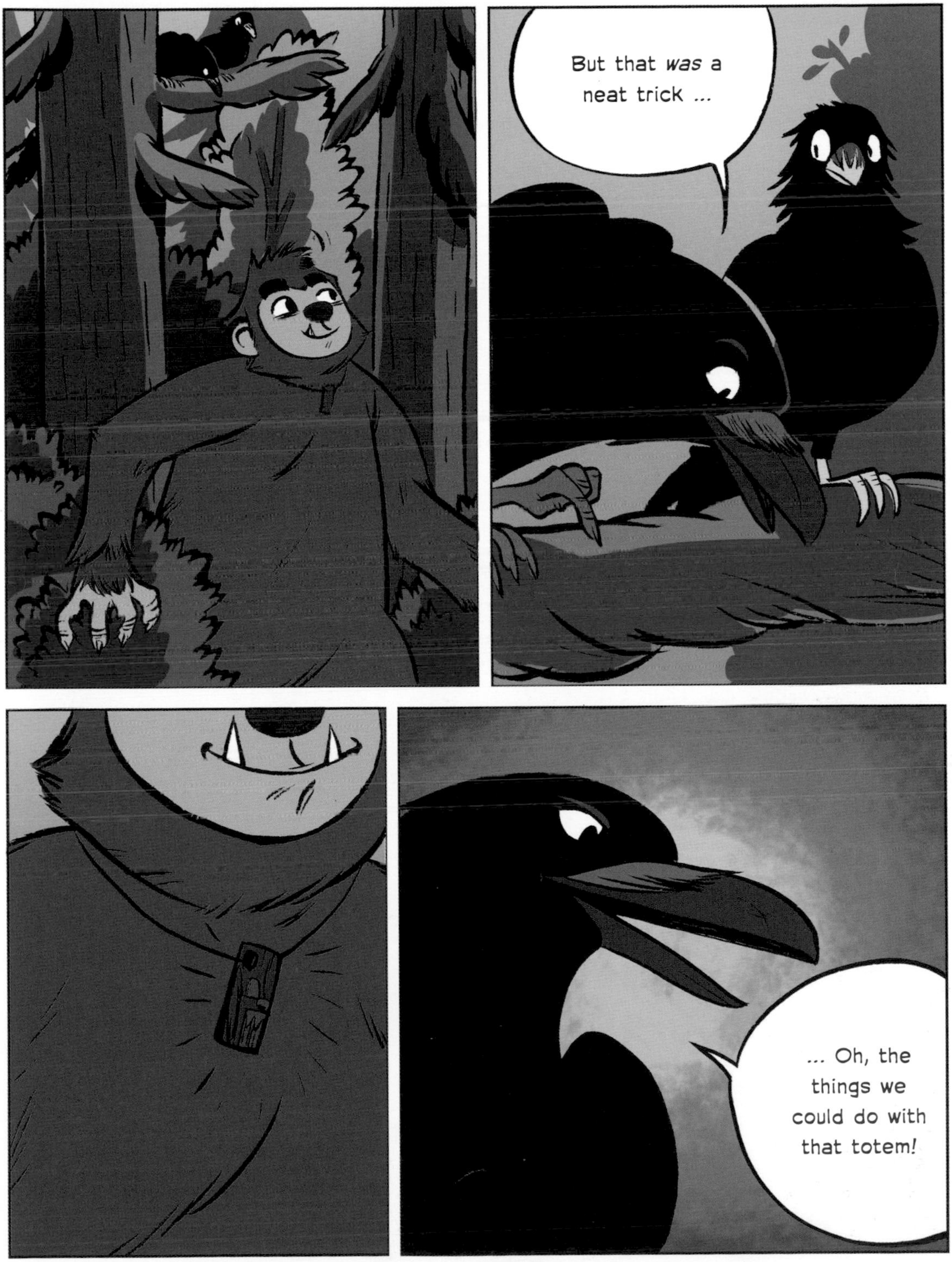
But that *was* a neat trick ...
... Oh, the things we could do with that totem!

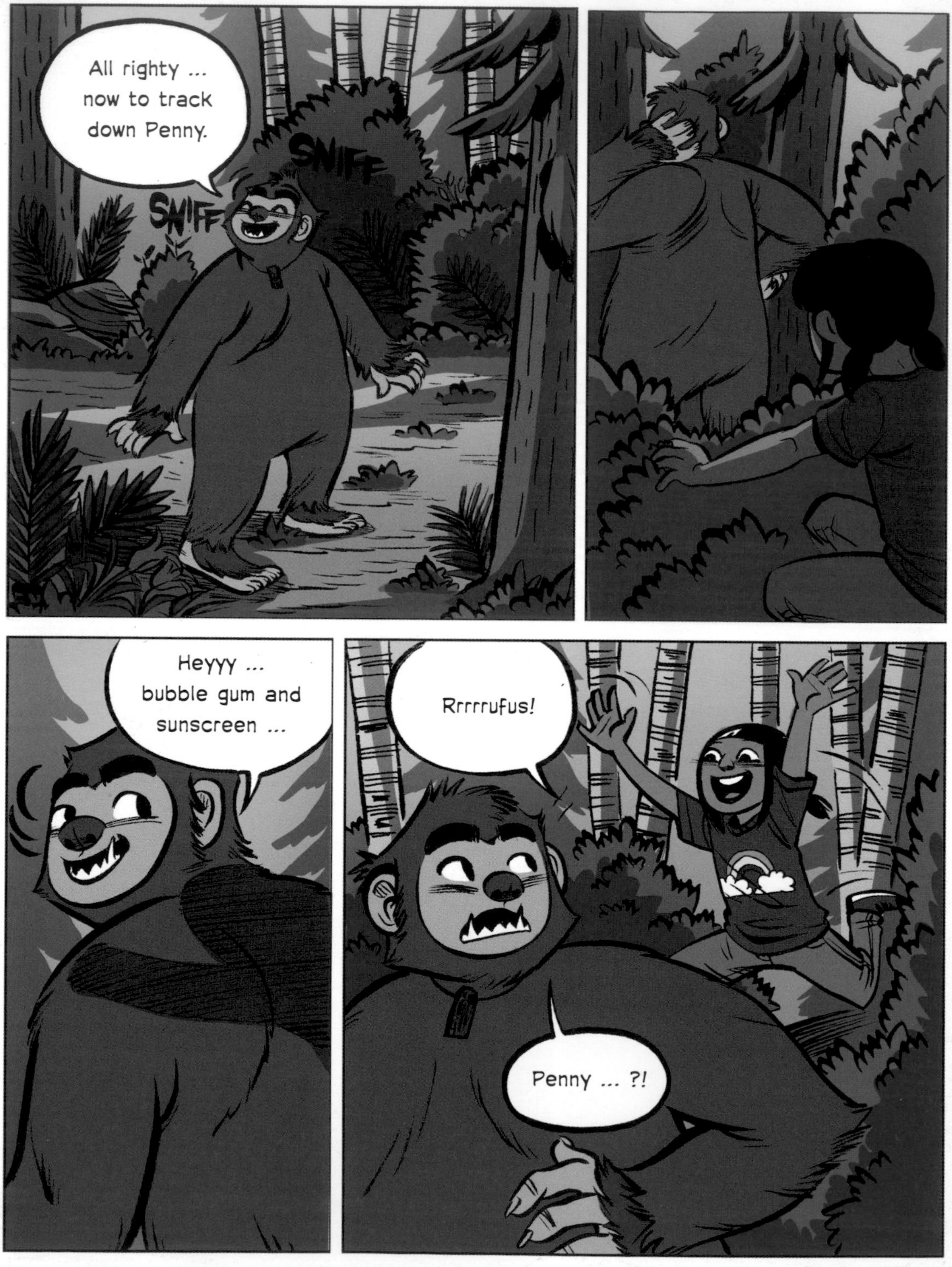
All righty ... now to track down Penny.
SNIFF
SNIFF
Heyyy ... bubble gum and sunscreen ...
Rrrrrufus!
Penny ... ?!

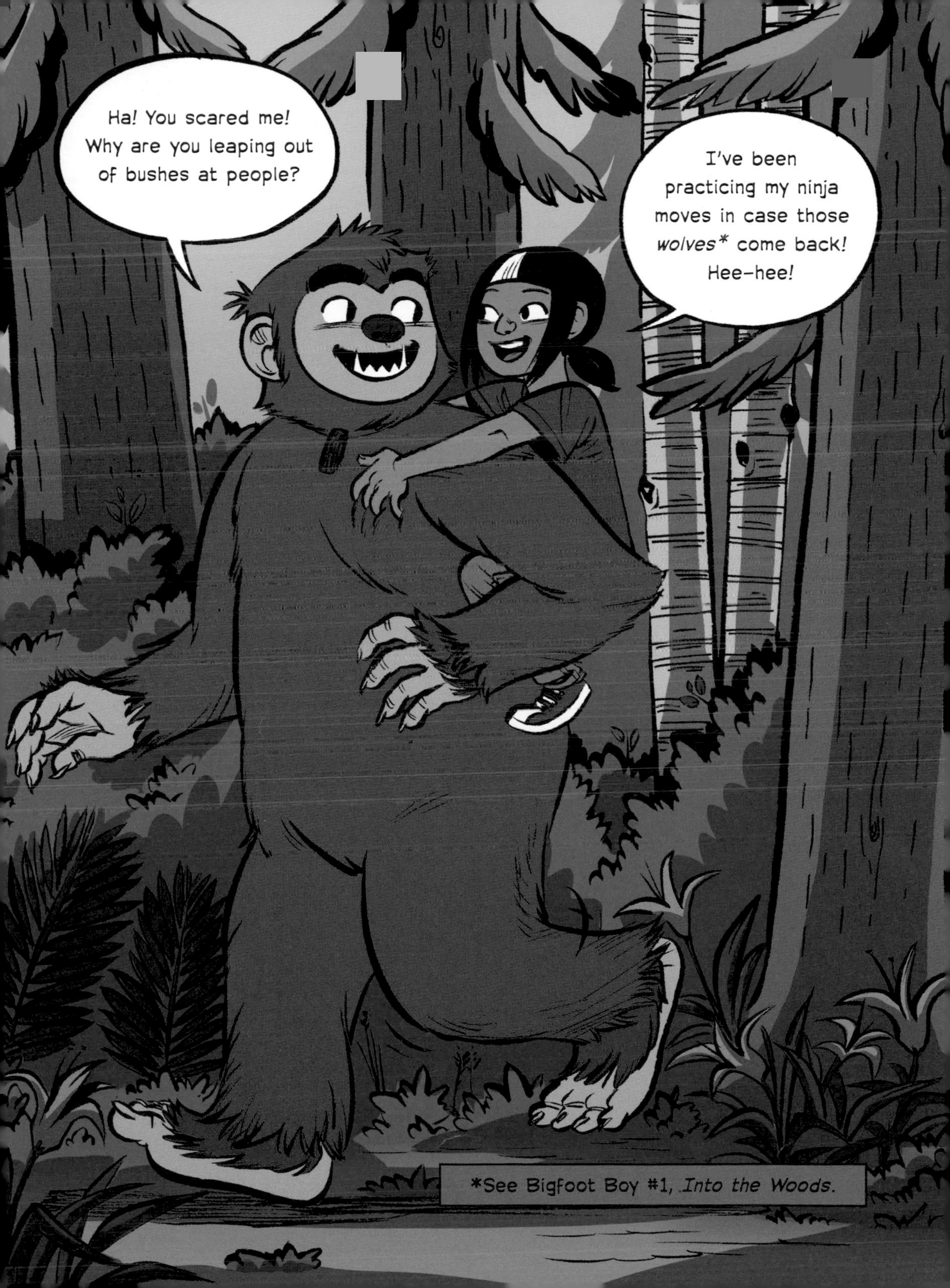
Ha! You scared me! Why are you leaping out of bushes at people?
I've been practicing my ninja moves in case those *wolves** come back! Hee-hee!
*See Bigfoot Boy #1, *Into the Woods.*

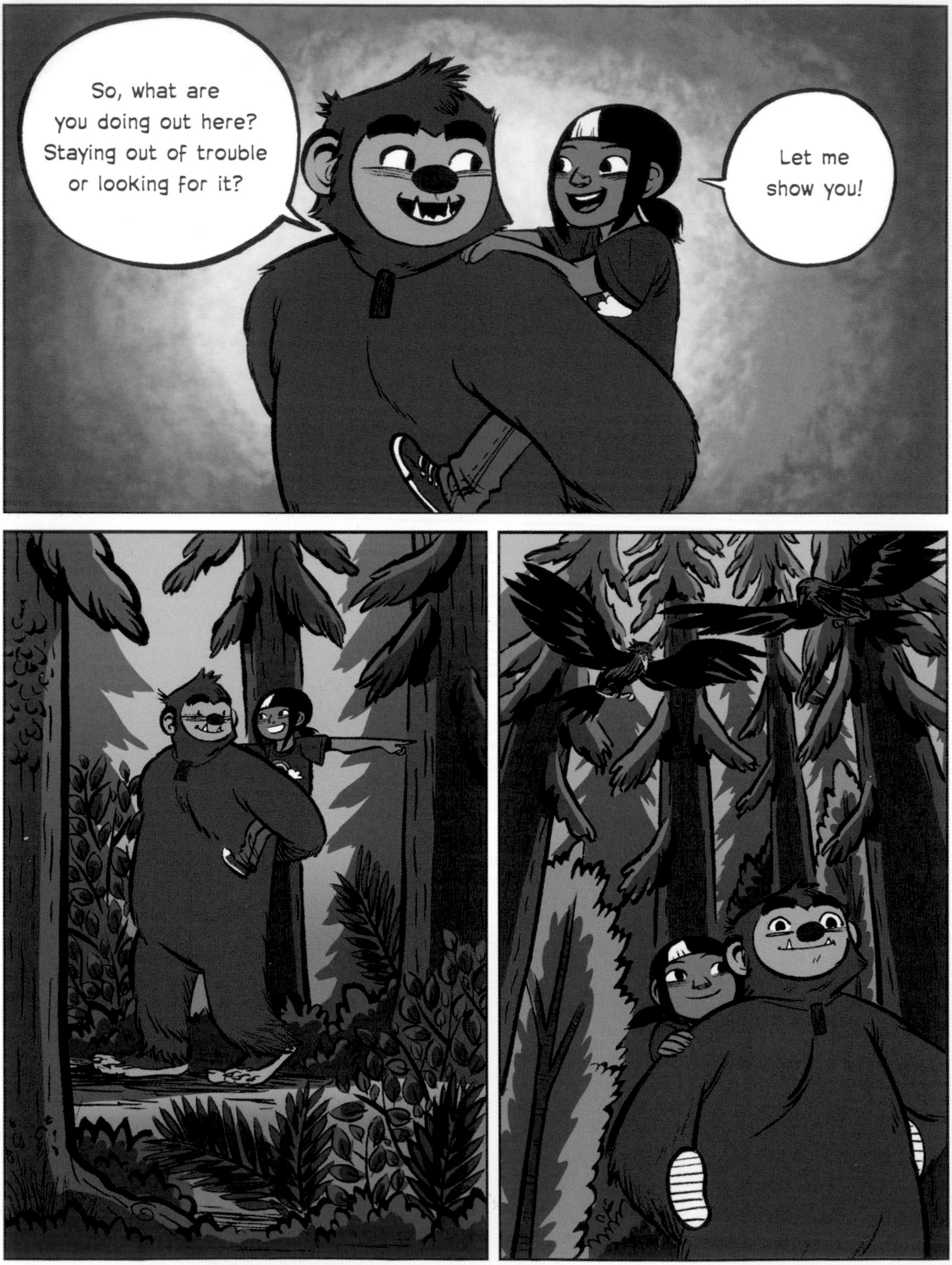
So, what are you doing out here? Staying out of trouble or looking for it?
Let me show you!

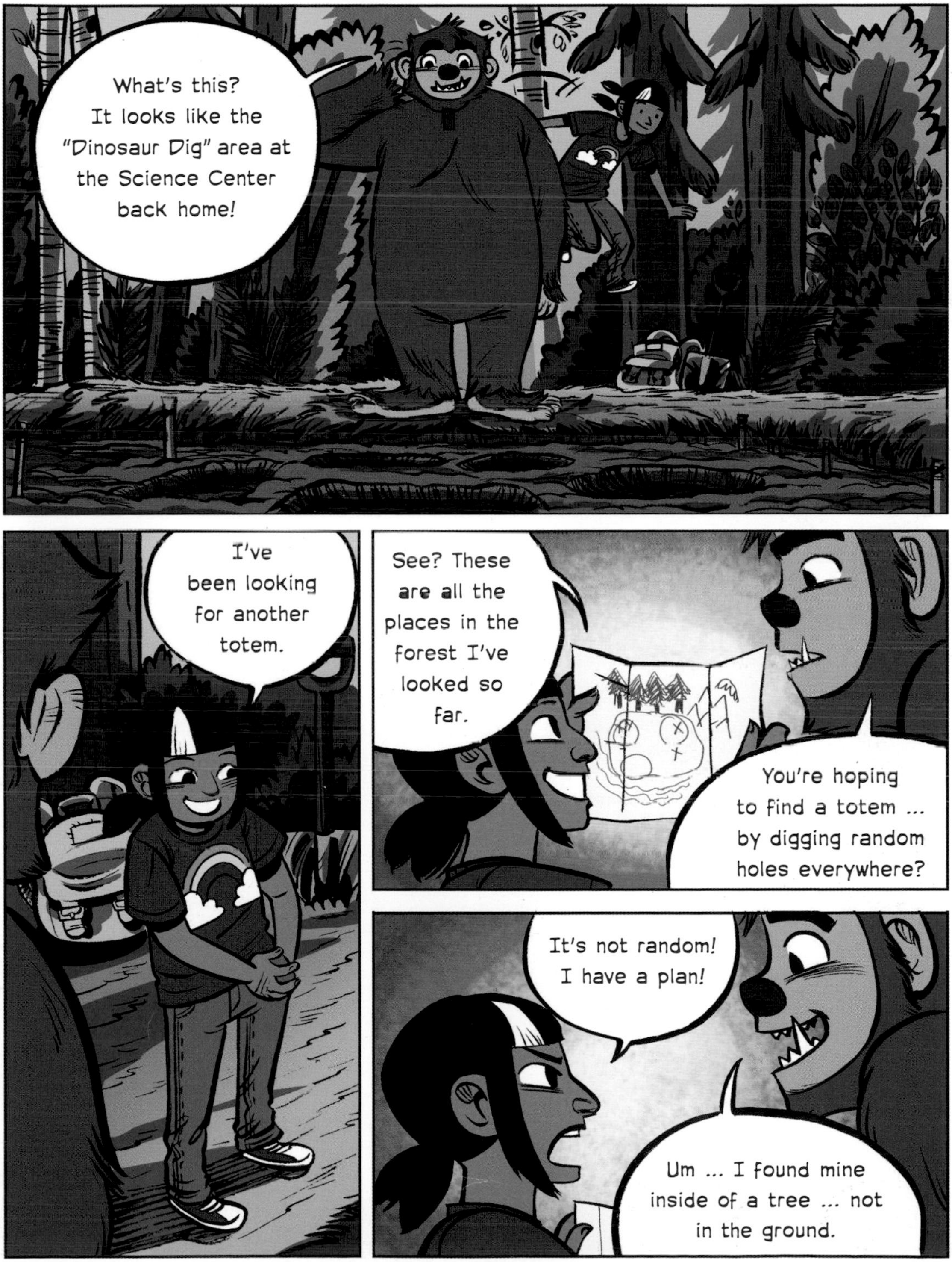
What's this?
It looks like the "Dinosaur Dig" area at the Science Center back home!
I've been looking for another totem.
See? These are all the places in the forest I've looked so far.
You're hoping to find a totem ... by digging random holes everywhere?
It's not random! I have a plan!
Um ... I found mine inside of a tree ... not in the ground.

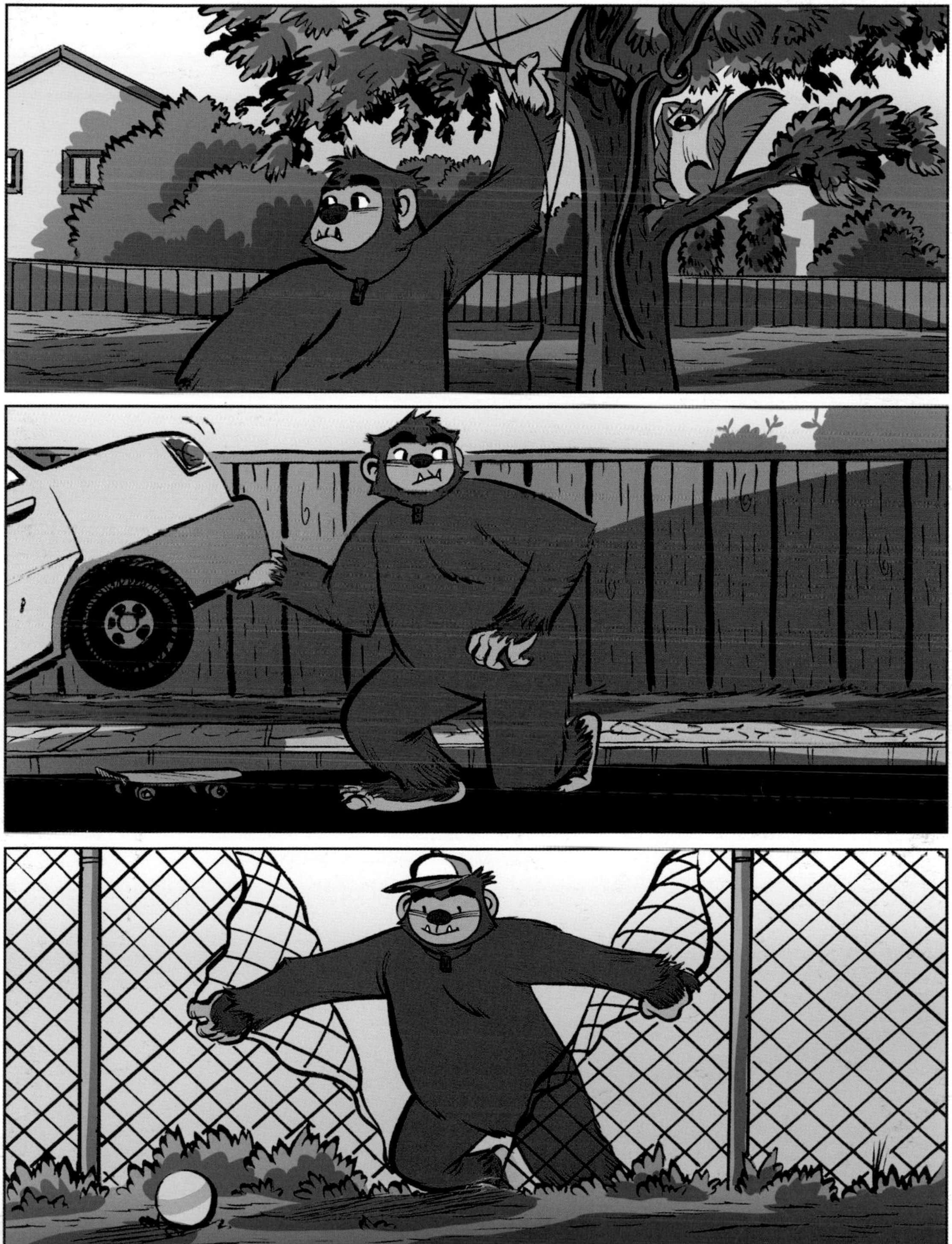

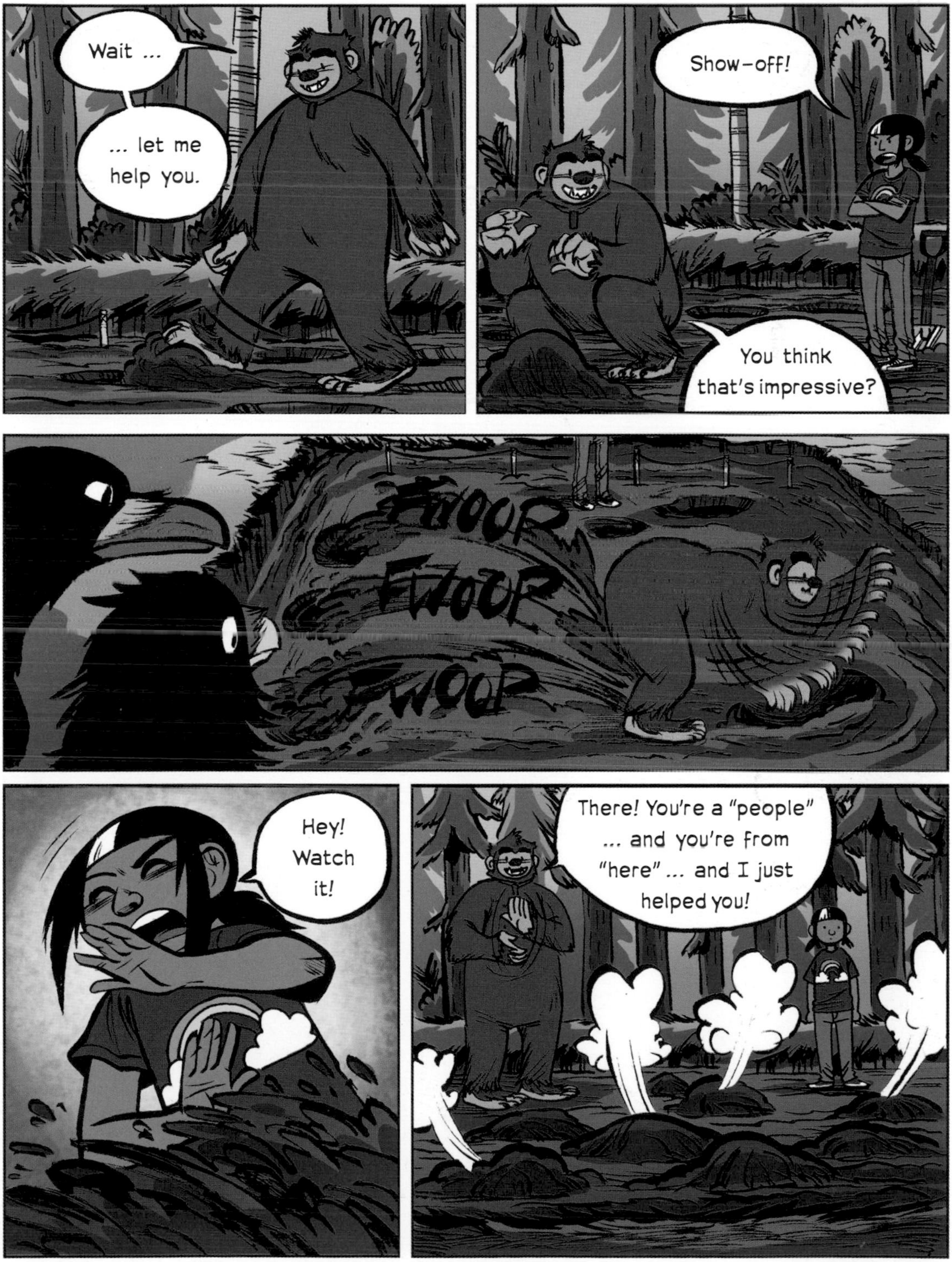
Wait ...
... let me help you.
Show-off!
You think that's impressive?
FWOOP
FWOOP
FWOOP
Hey! Watch it!
There! You're a "people" ... and you're from "here" ... and I just helped you!

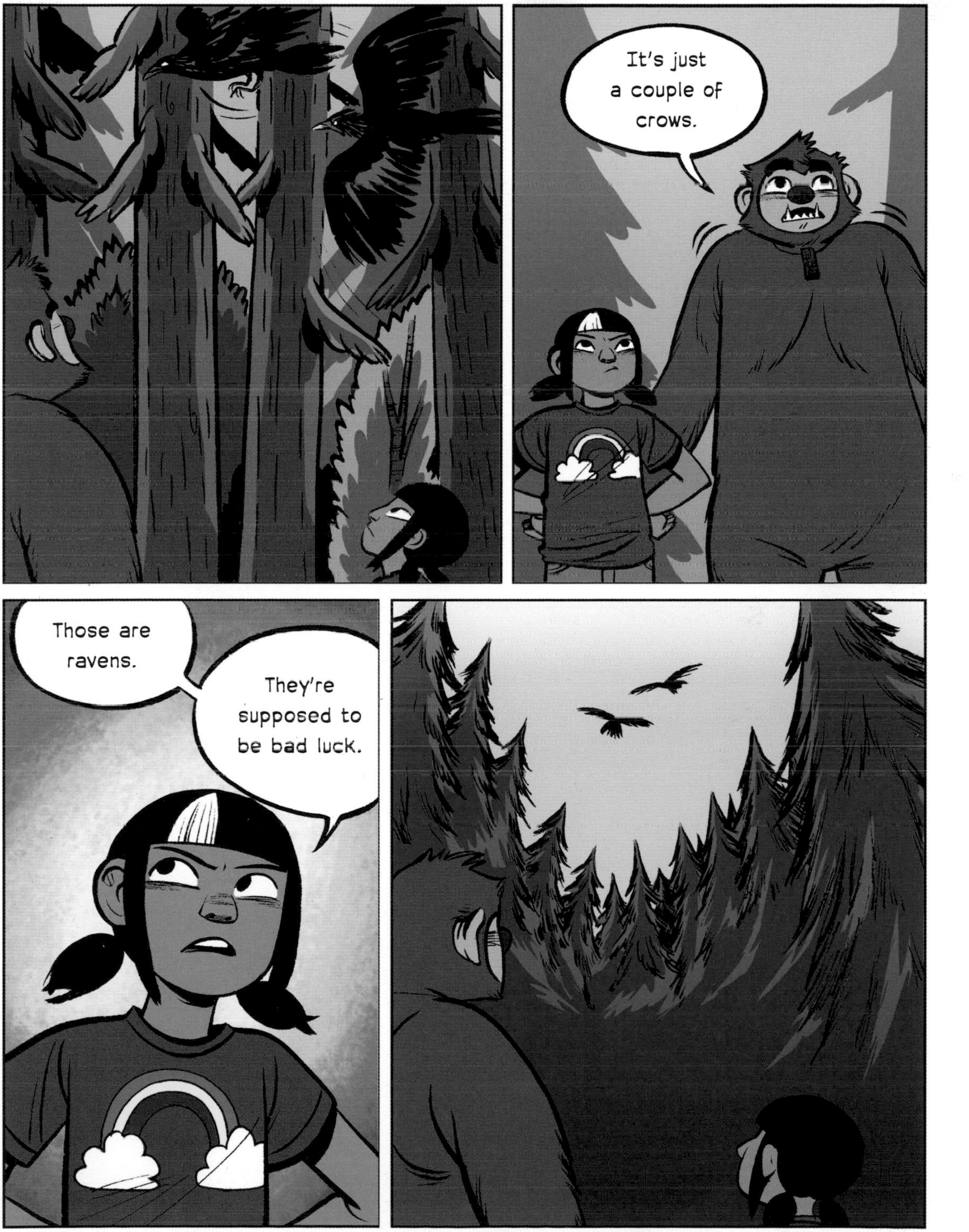
It's just a couple of crows.
Those are ravens.
They're supposed to be bad luck.

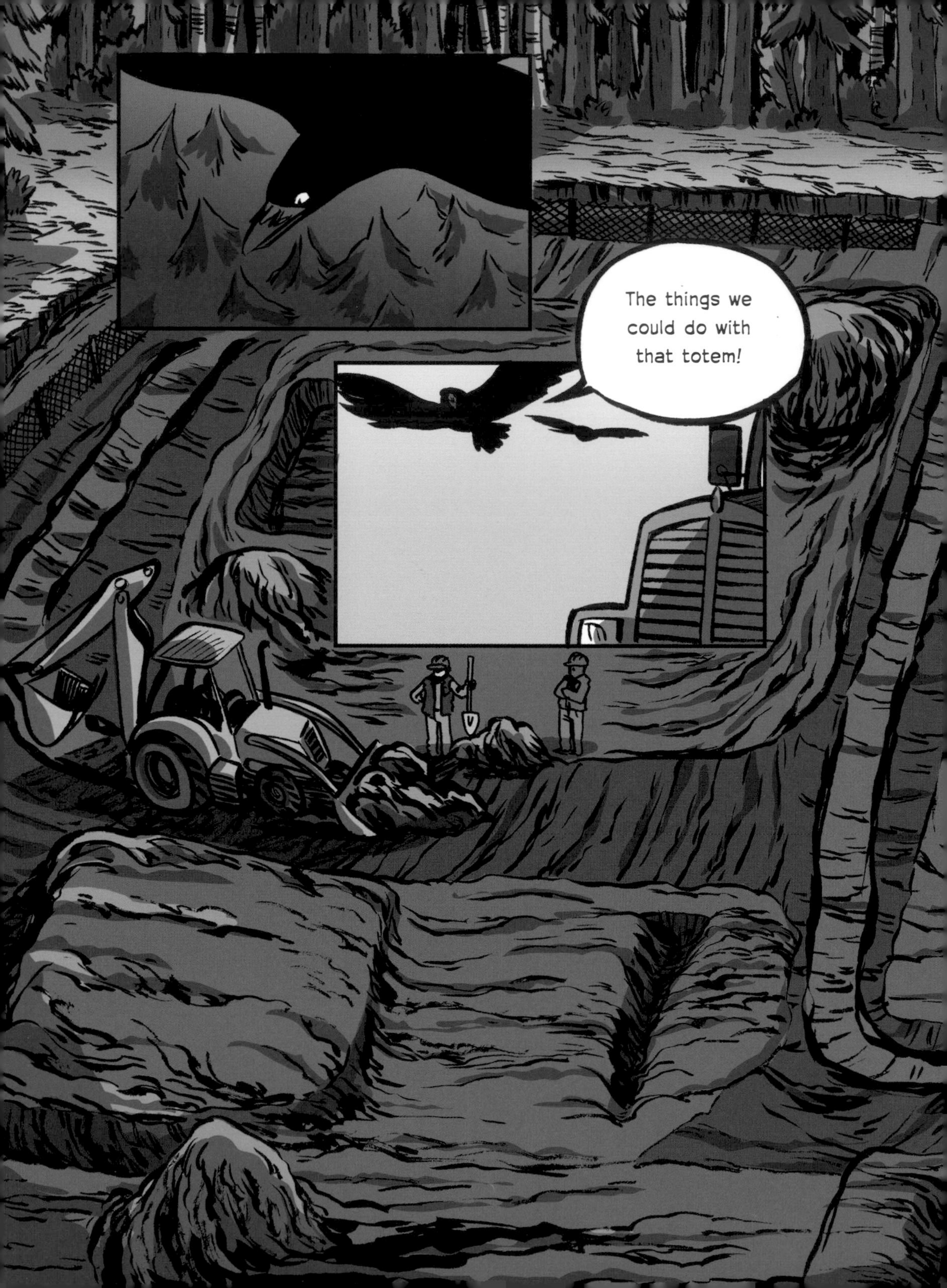
The things we could do with that totem!

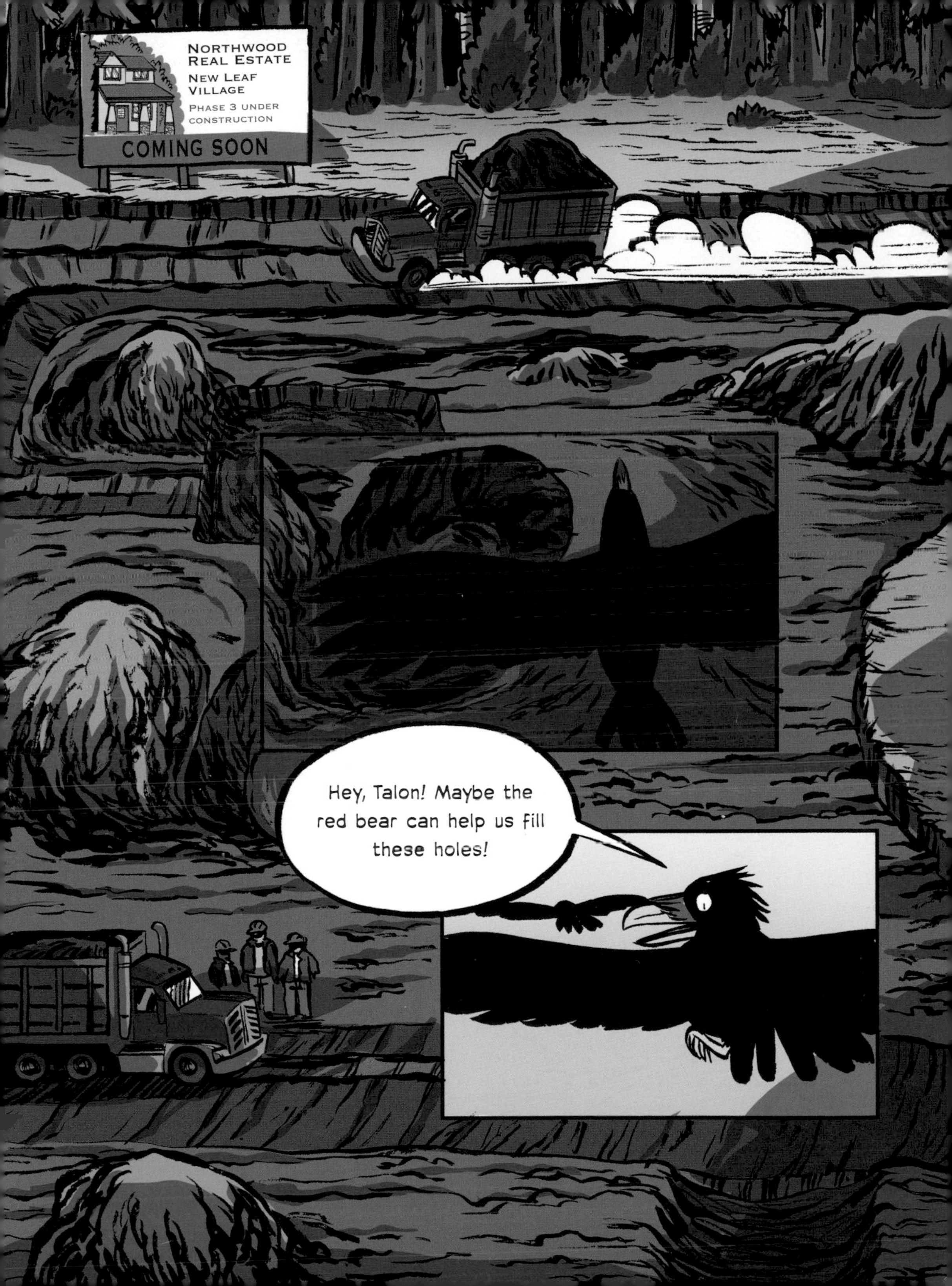
NORTHWOOD REAL ESTATE
NEW LEAF VILLAGE
PHASE 3 UNDER CONSTRUCTION
COMING SOON
Hey, Talon! Maybe the red bear can help us fill these holes!

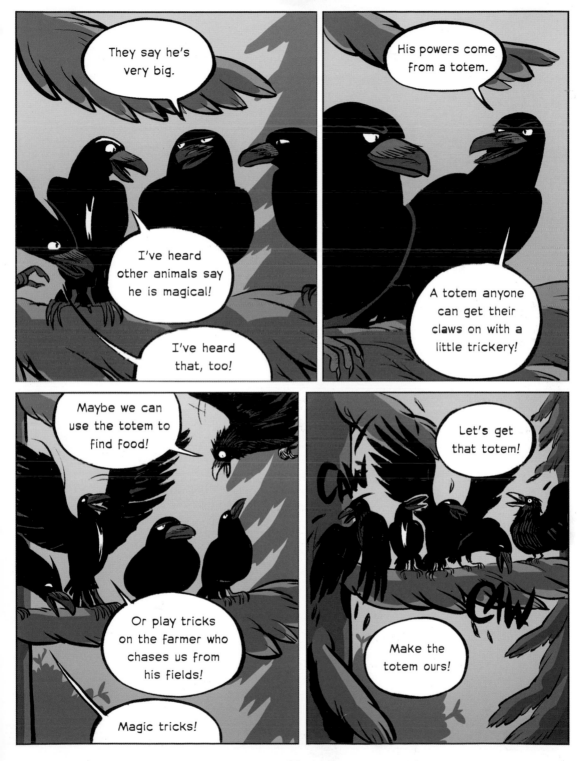

41

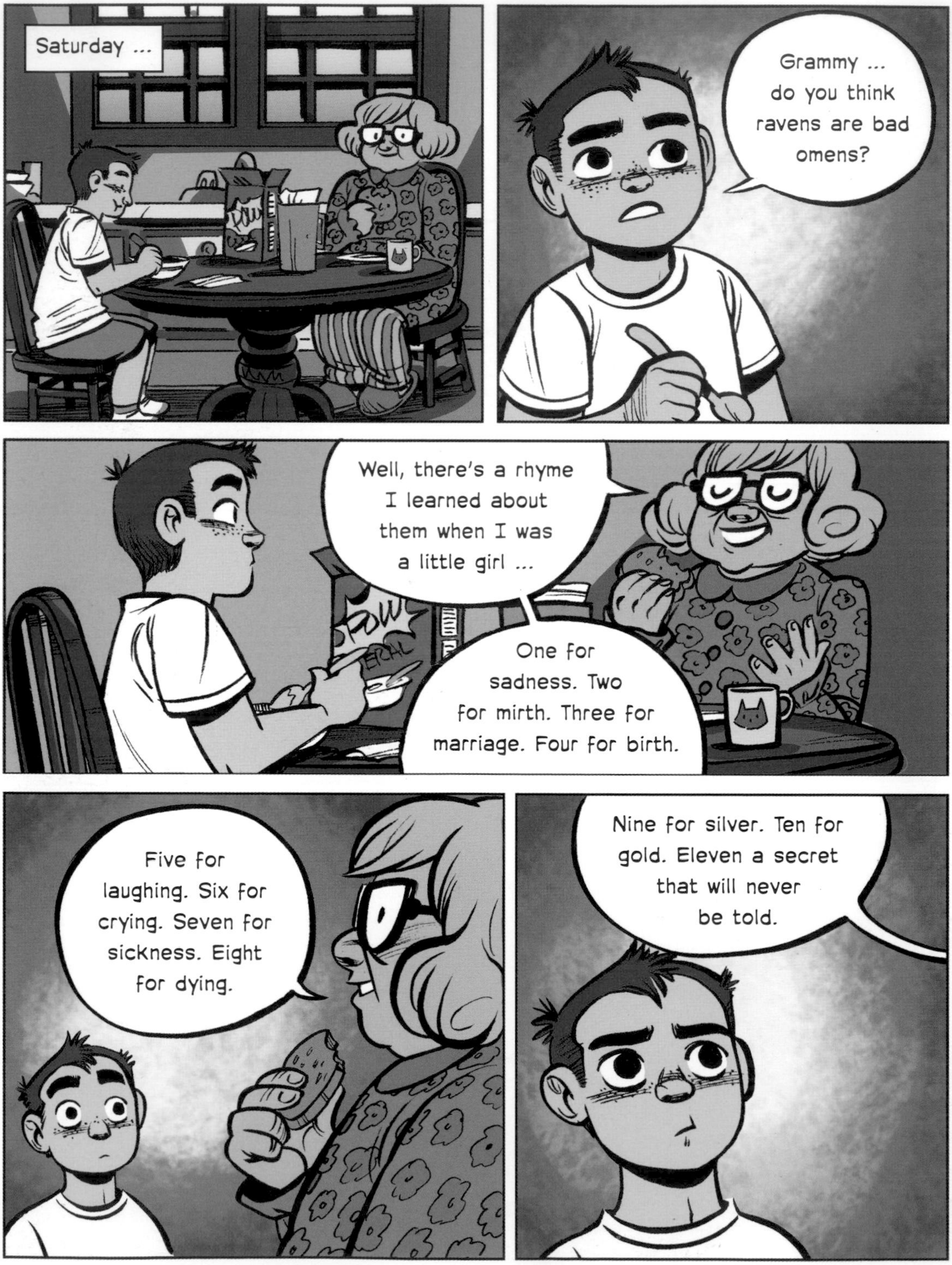
Saturday ...
Grammy ... do you think ravens are bad omens?
Well, there's a rhyme I learned about them when I was a little girl ...
One for sadness. Two for mirth. Three for marriage. Four for birth.
Five for laughing. Six for crying. Seven for sickness. Eight for dying.
Nine for silver. Ten for gold. Eleven a secret that will never be told.

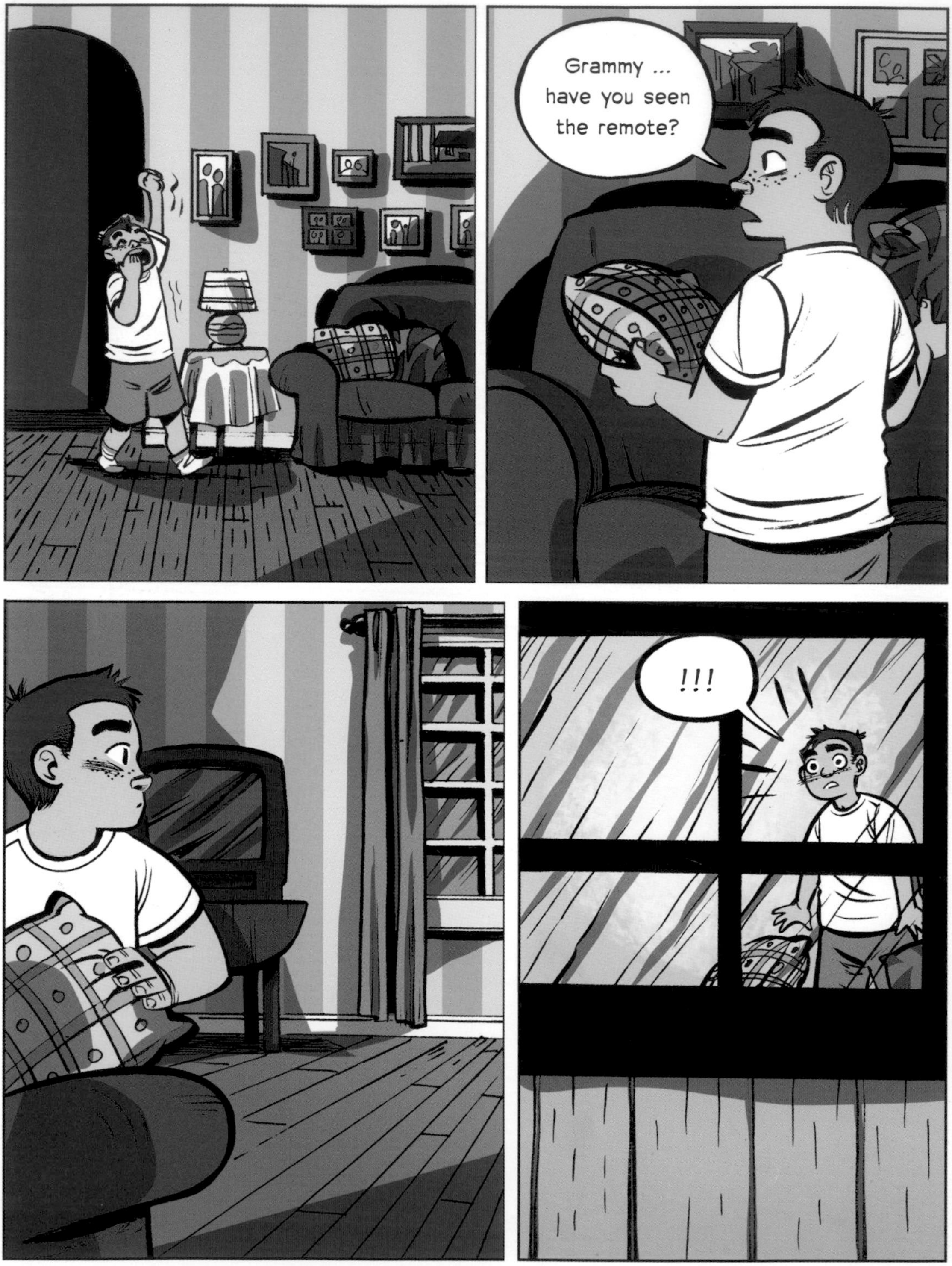
Grammy ...
have you seen
the remote?
!!!

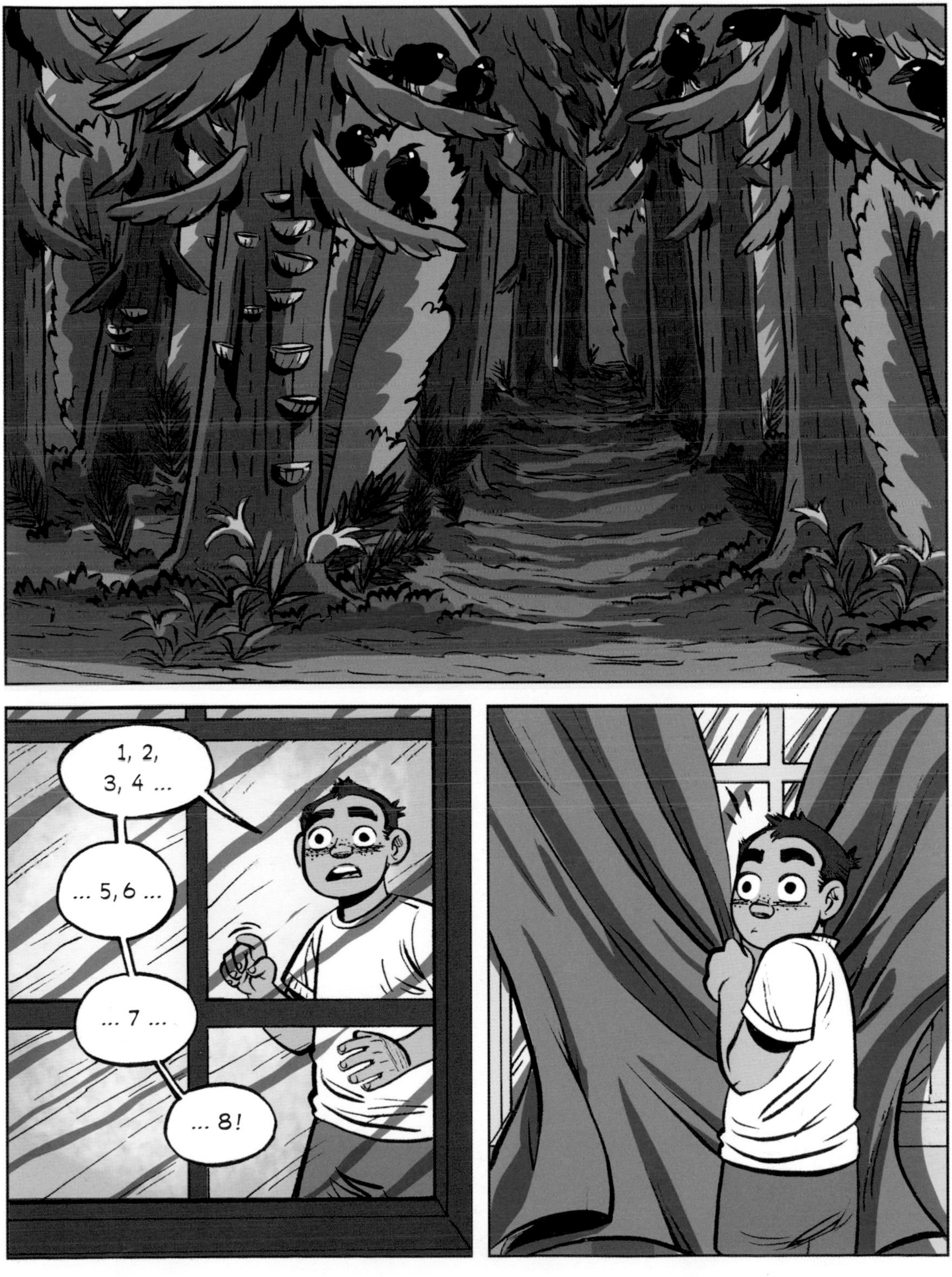
1, 2,
3, 4 ...
... 5, 6 ...
... 7 ...
... 8!

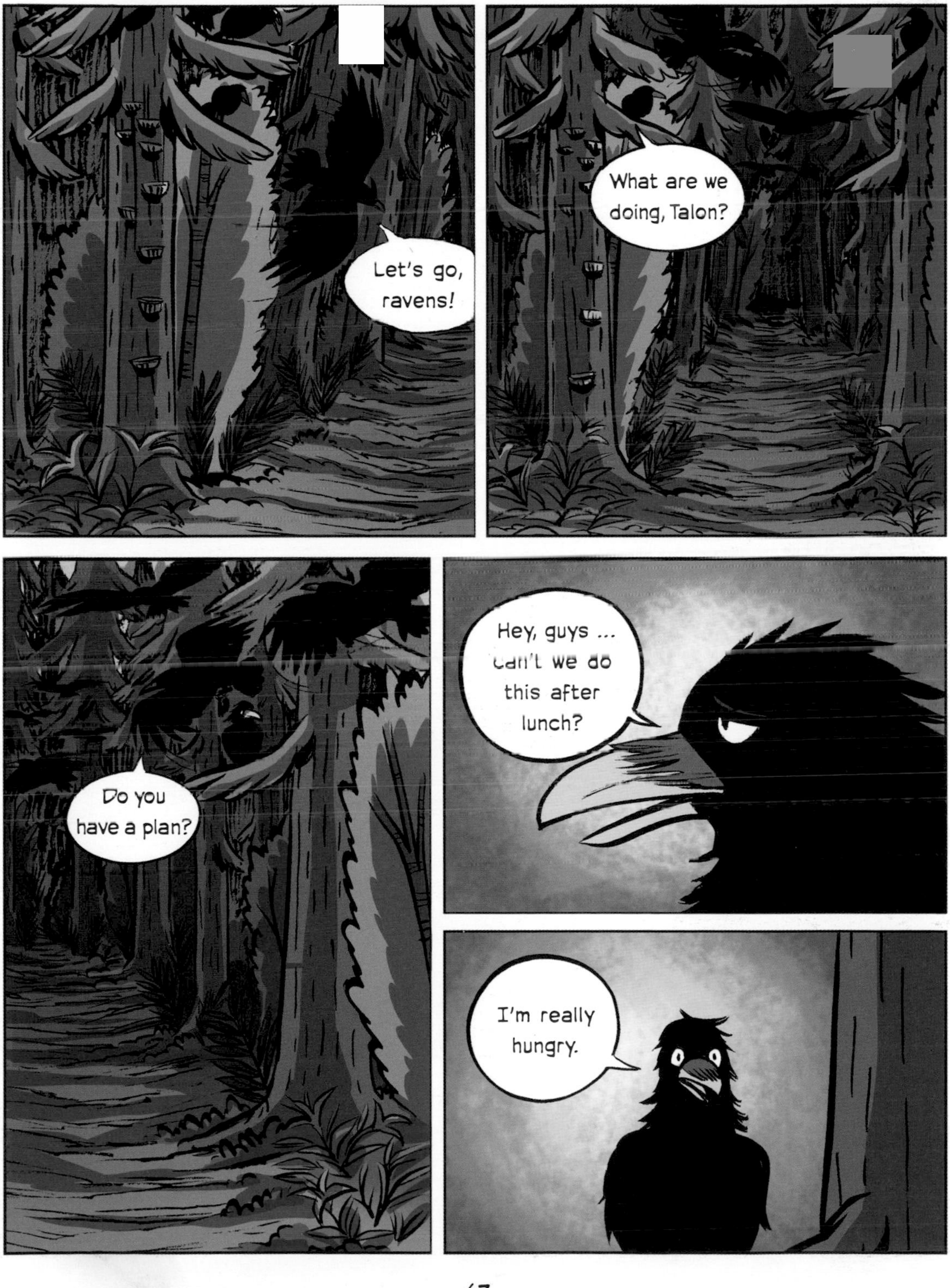
Let's go, ravens!
What are we doing, Talon?
Do you have a plan?
Hey, guys ... can't we do this after lunch?
I'm really hungry.

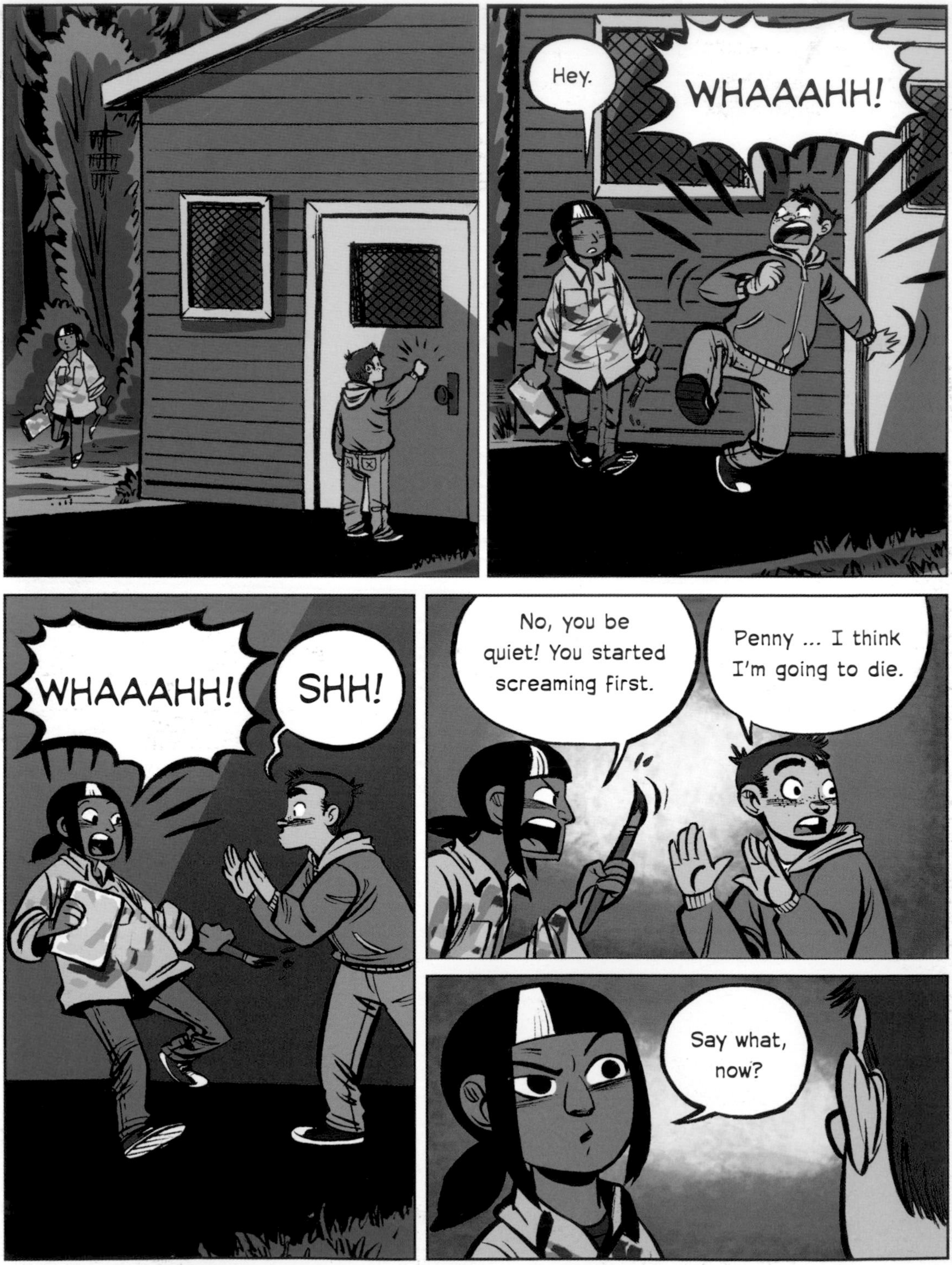
Hey.
WHAAAHH!
WHAAAHH!
SHH!
No, you be quiet! You started screaming first.
Penny ... I think I'm going to die.
Say what, now?

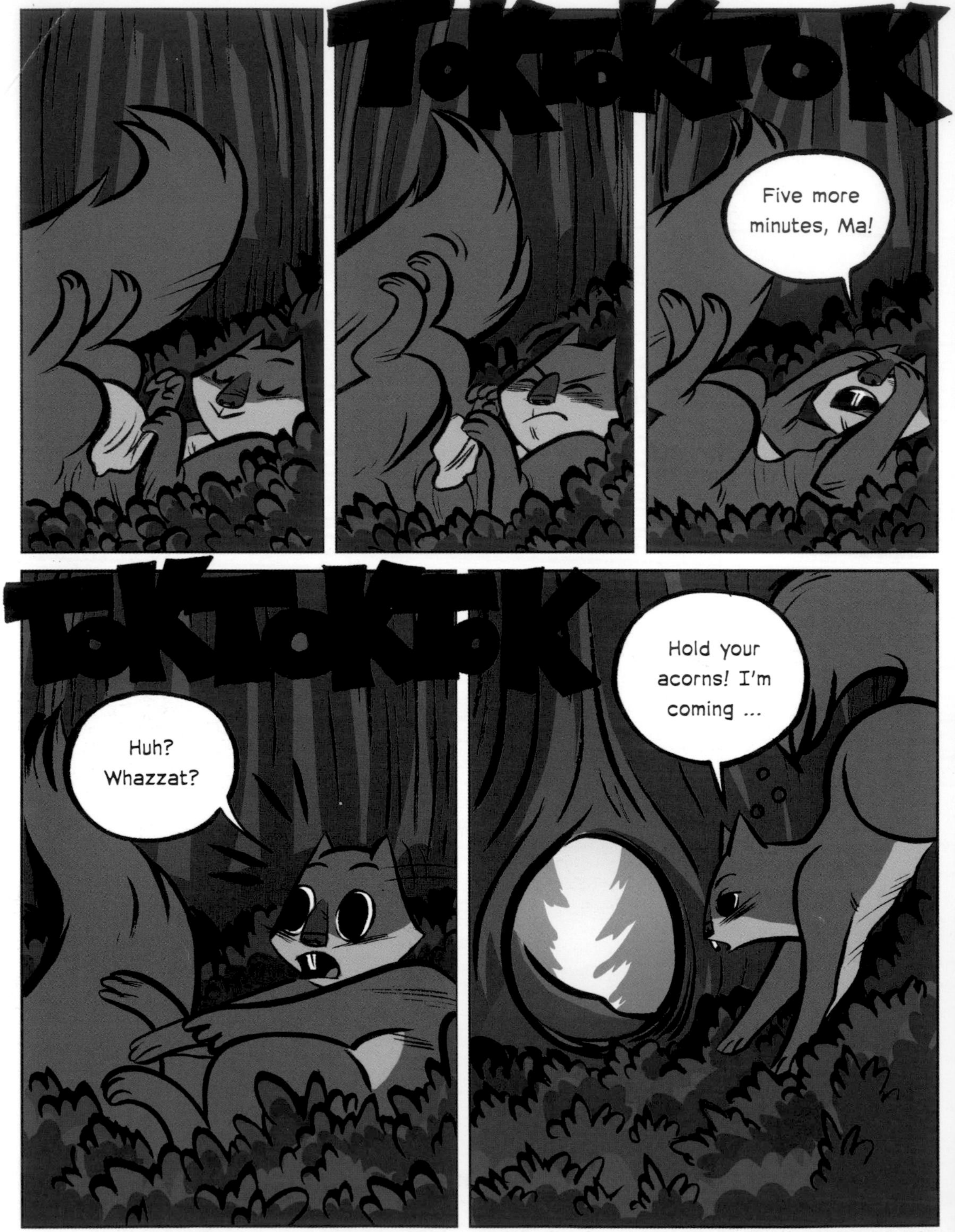
TOKTOKTOK
Five more minutes, Ma!
TOKTOKTOK
Huh? Whazzat?
Hold your acorns! I'm coming ...

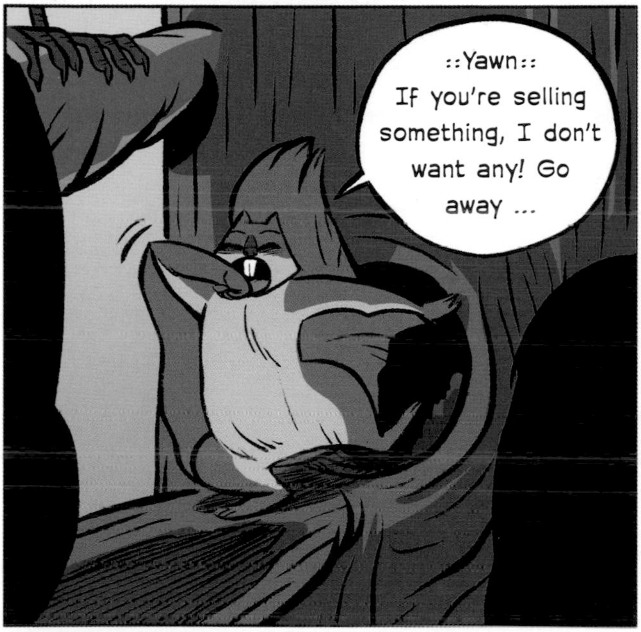
::Yawn:: If you're selling something, I don't want any! Go away ...

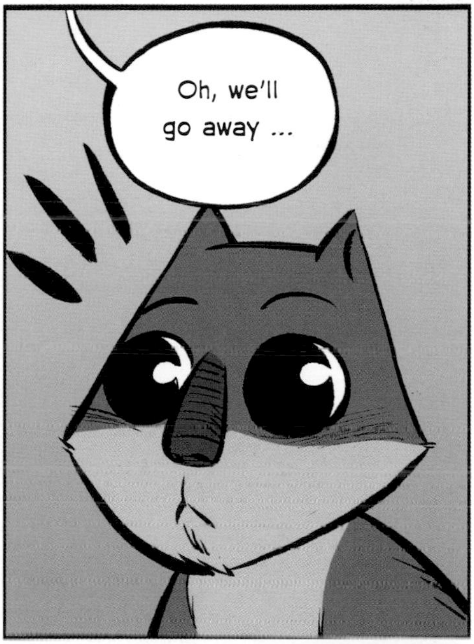
Oh, we'll go away ...

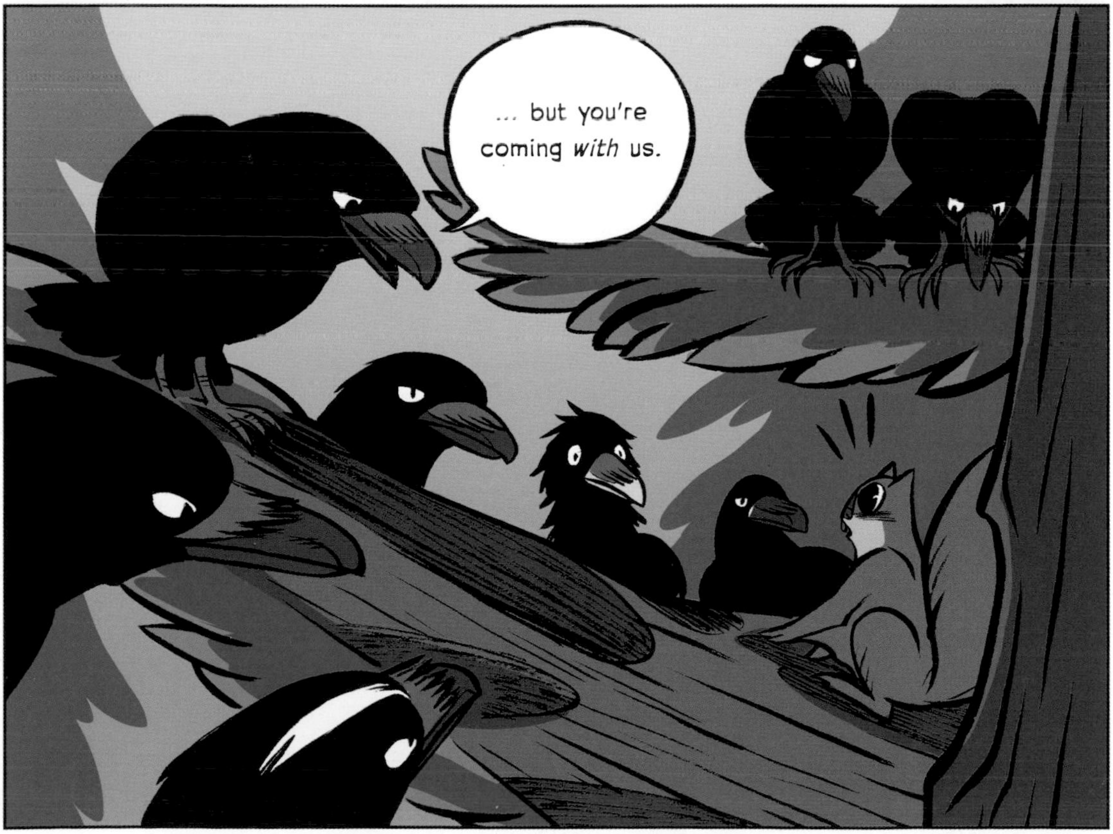
... but you're coming *with* us.

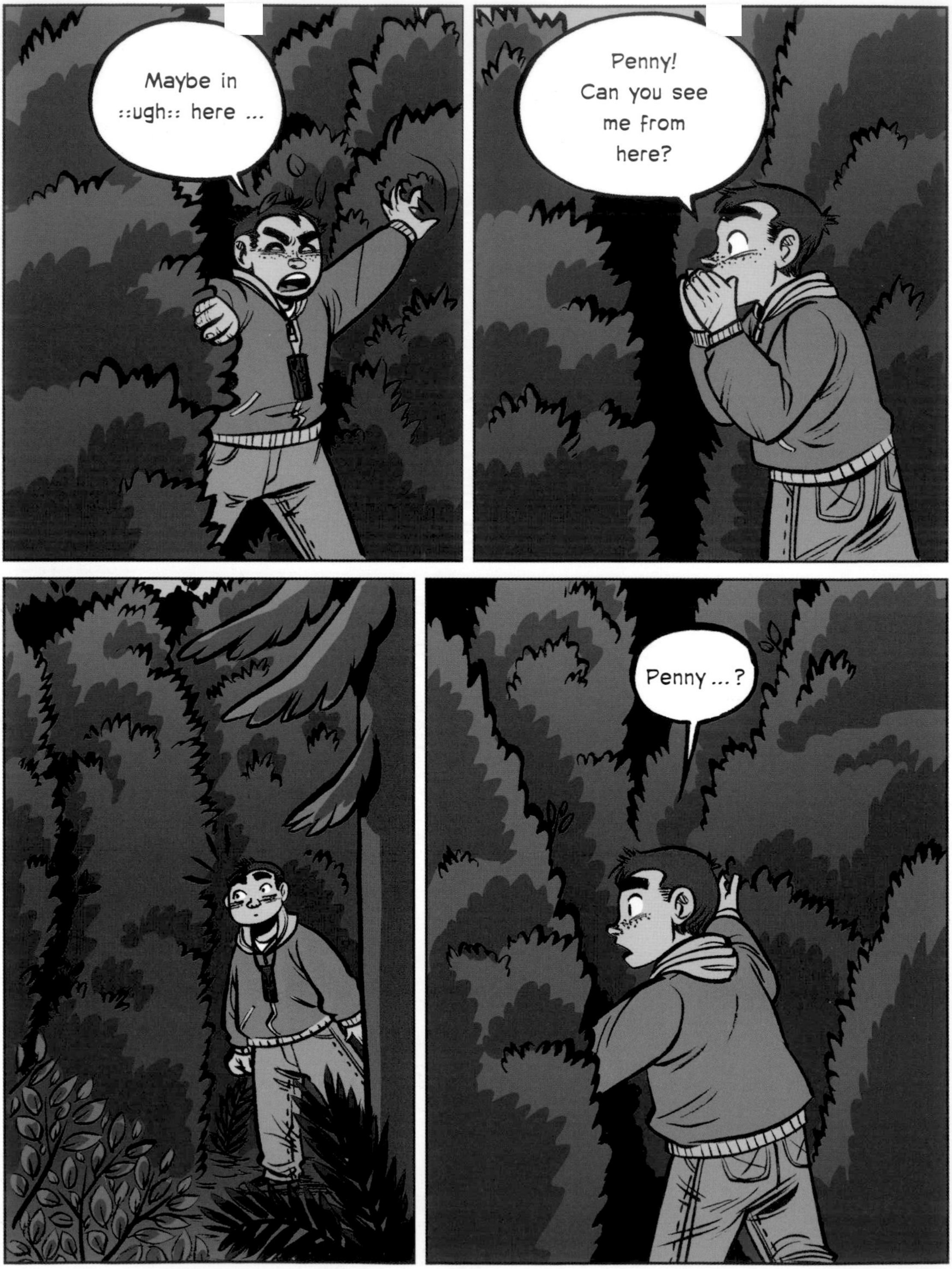
Maybe in ::ugh:: here ...
Penny! Can you see me from here?
Penny ... ?

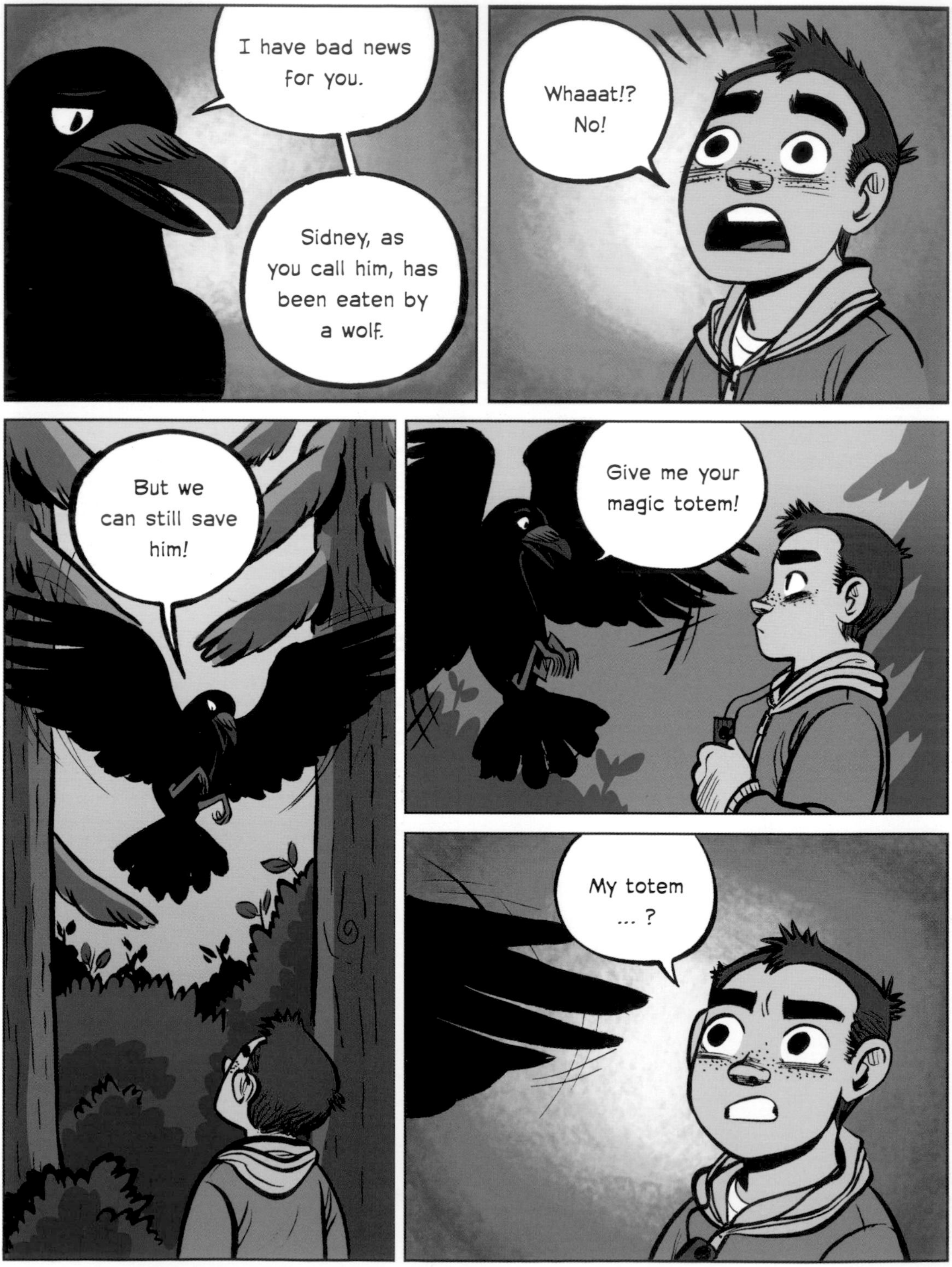
I have bad news for you.
Sidney, as you call him, has been eaten by a wolf.
Whaaat!? No!
But we can still save him!
Give me your magic totem!
My totem ... ?

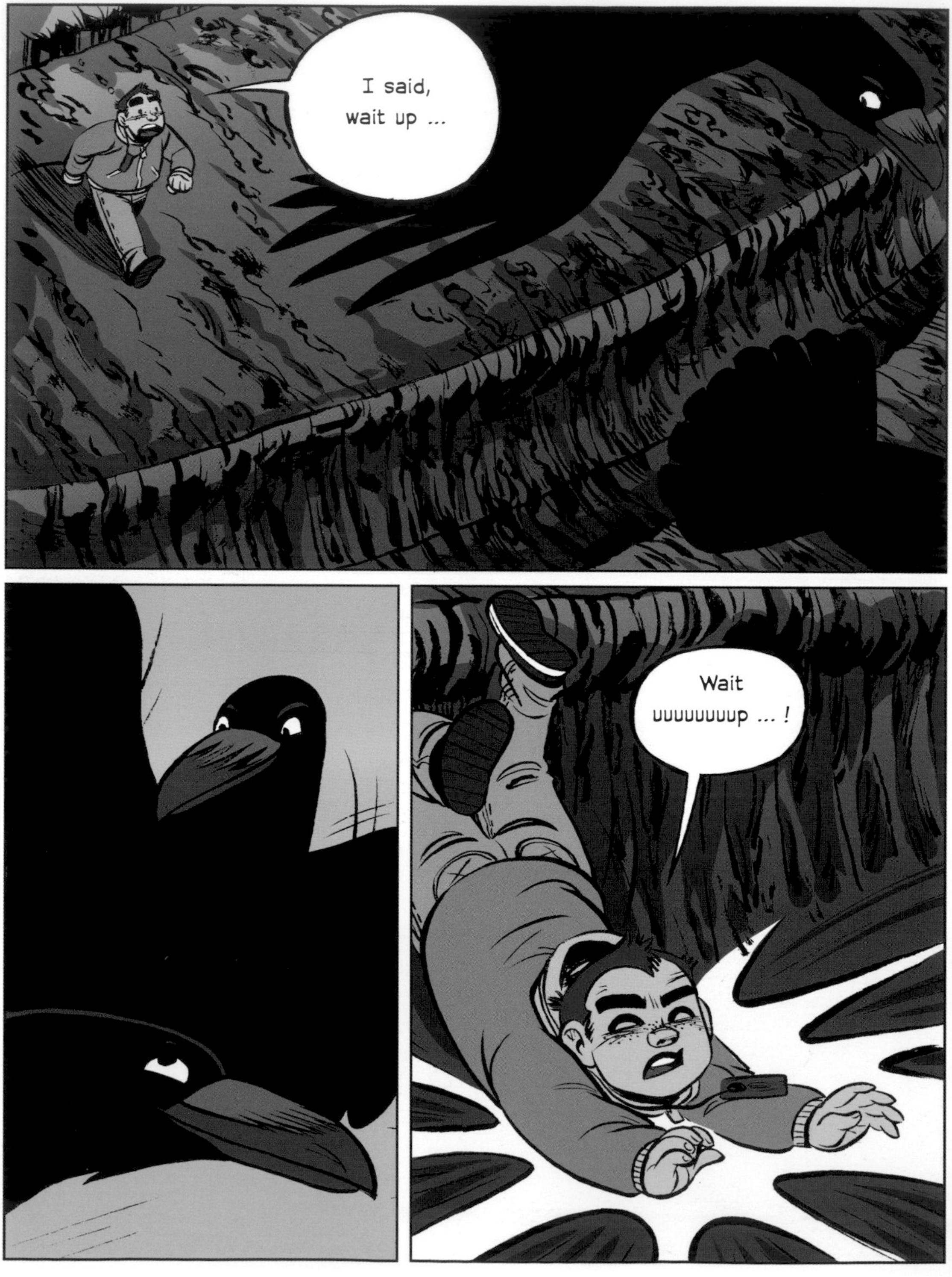
I said, wait up ...
Wait uuuuuuuup ... !

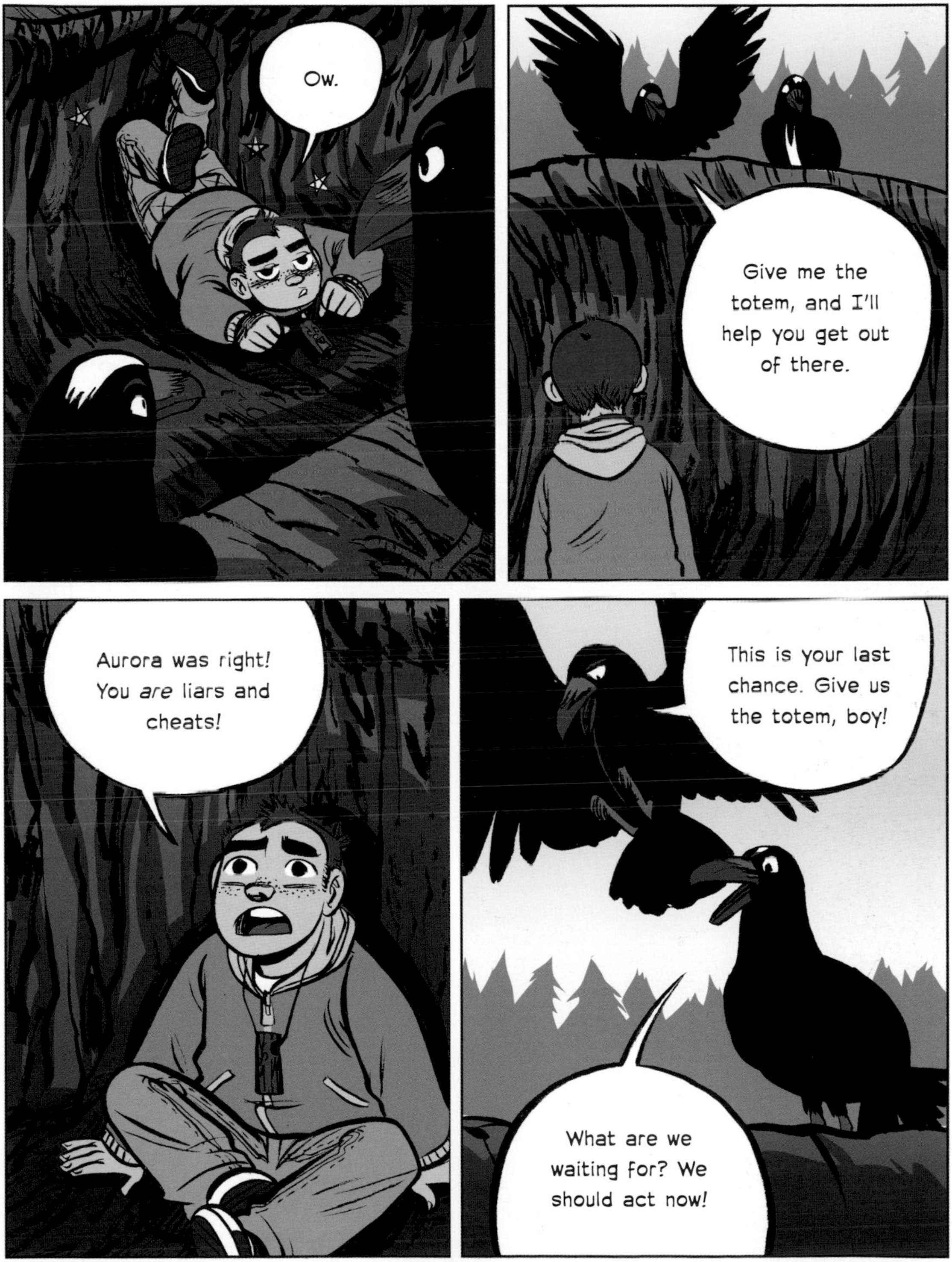
Ow.
Give me the totem, and I'll help you get out of there.
Aurora was right! You *are* liars and cheats!
This is your last chance. Give us the totem, boy!
What are we waiting for? We should act now!

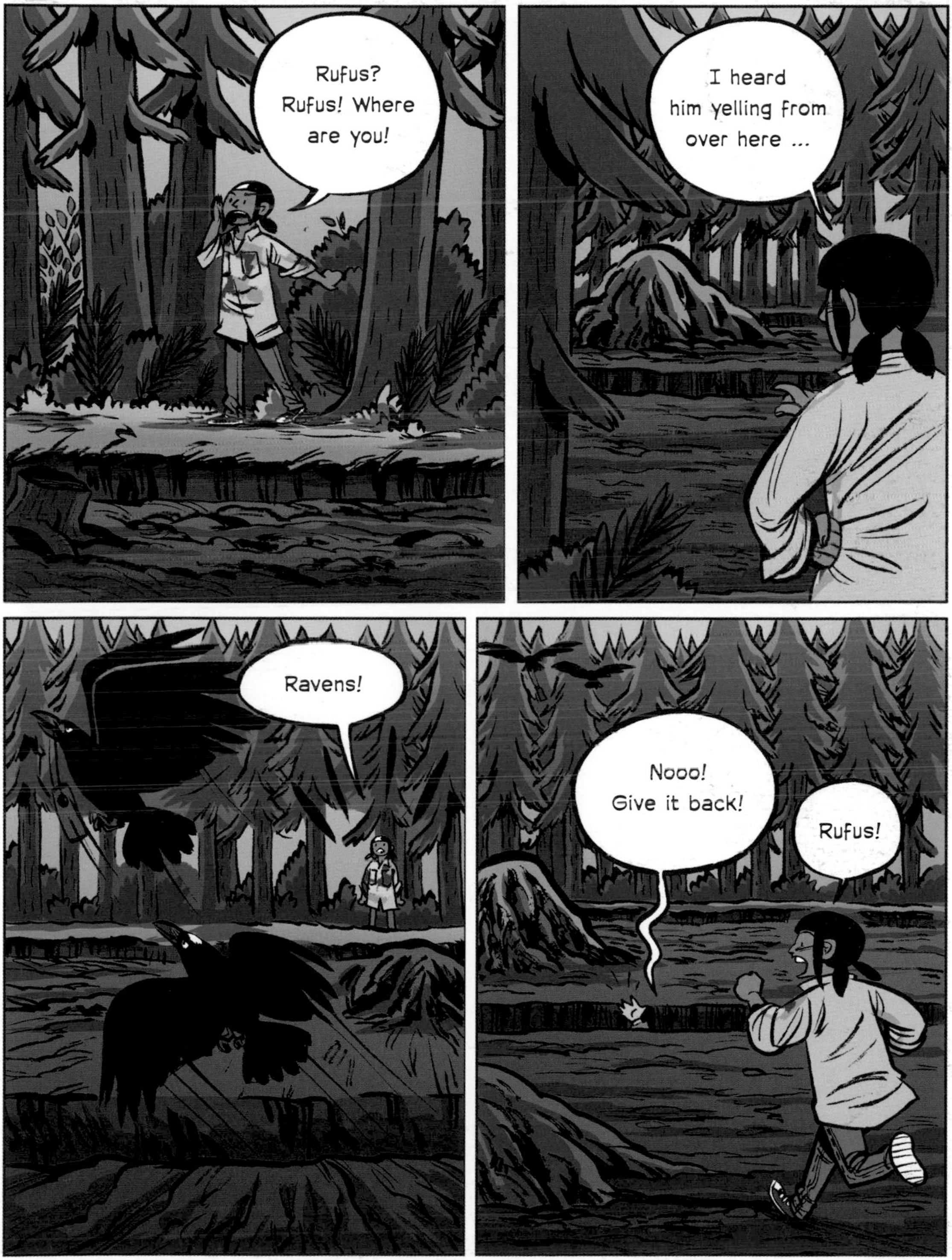
Rufus? Rufus! Where are you!
I heard him yelling from over here ...
Ravens!
Nooo! Give it back!
Rufus!

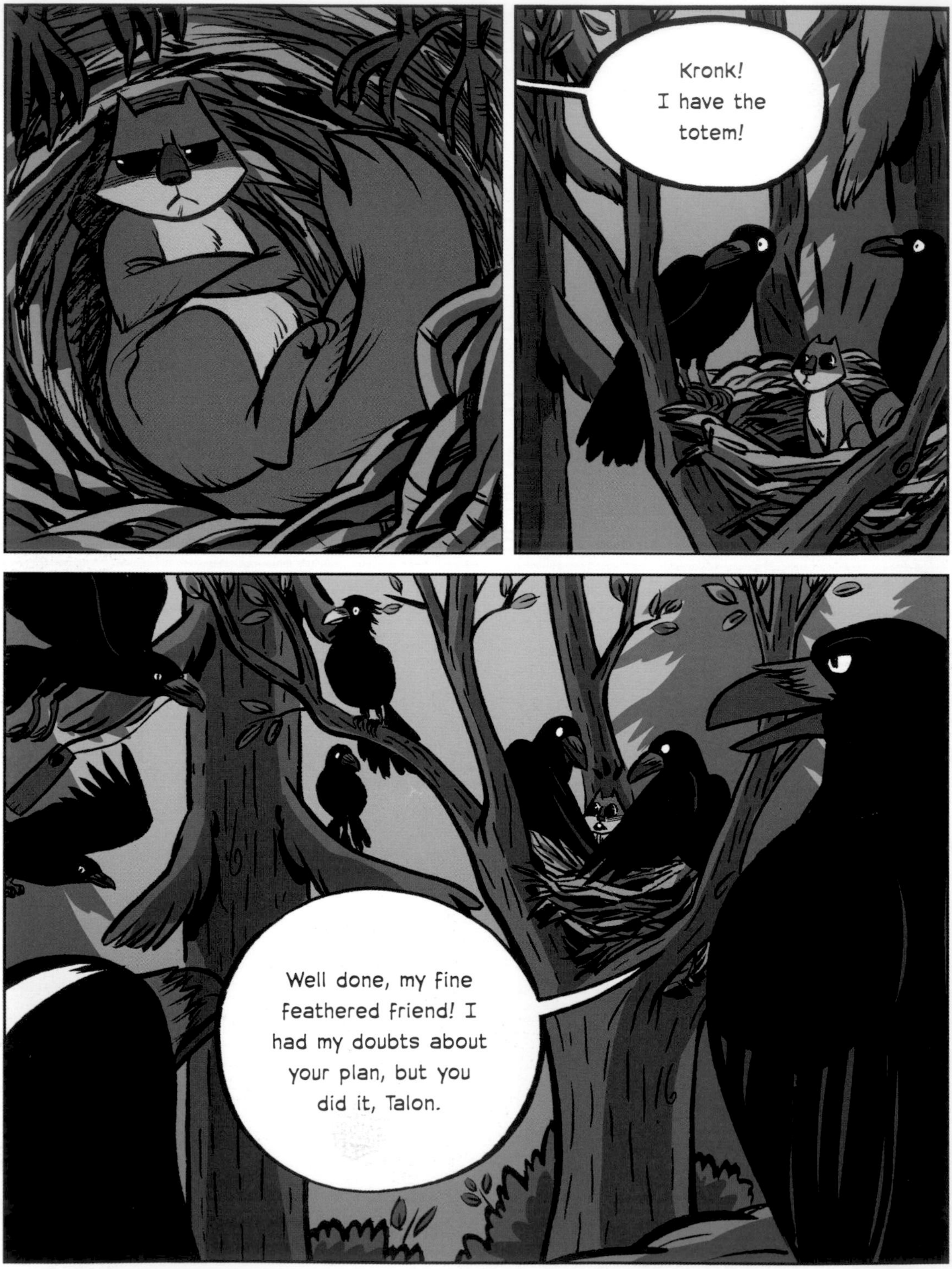
Kronk! I have the totem!
Well done, my fine feathered friend! I had my doubts about your plan, but you did it, Talon.

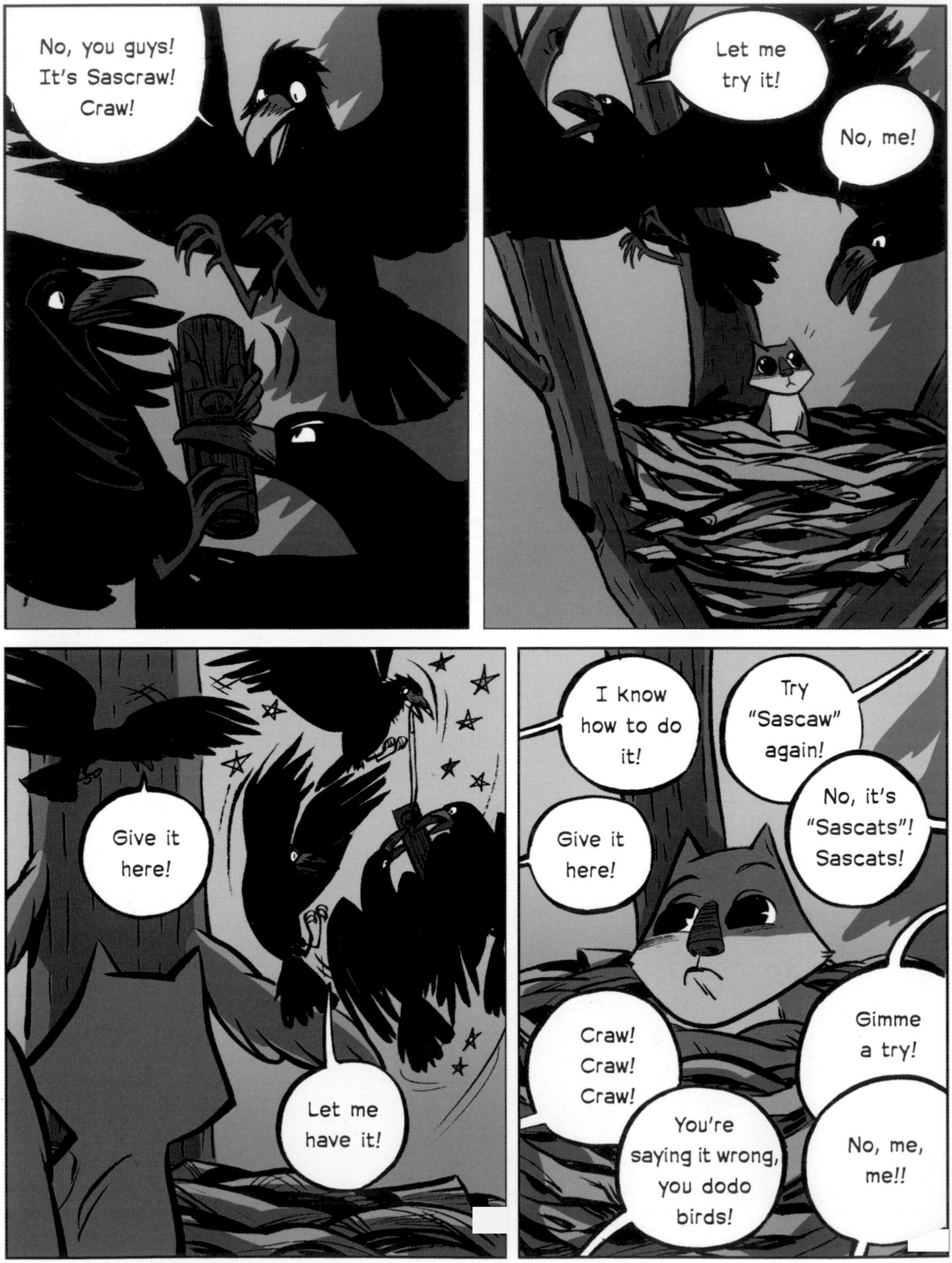
No, you guys! It's Sascraw! Craw!
Let me try it!
No, me!
Give it here!
Let me have it!
I know how to do it!
Try "Sascaw" again!
Give it here!
No, it's "Sascats"! Sascats!
Craw! Craw! Craw!
Gimme a try!
You're saying it wrong, you dodo birds!
No, me, me!!

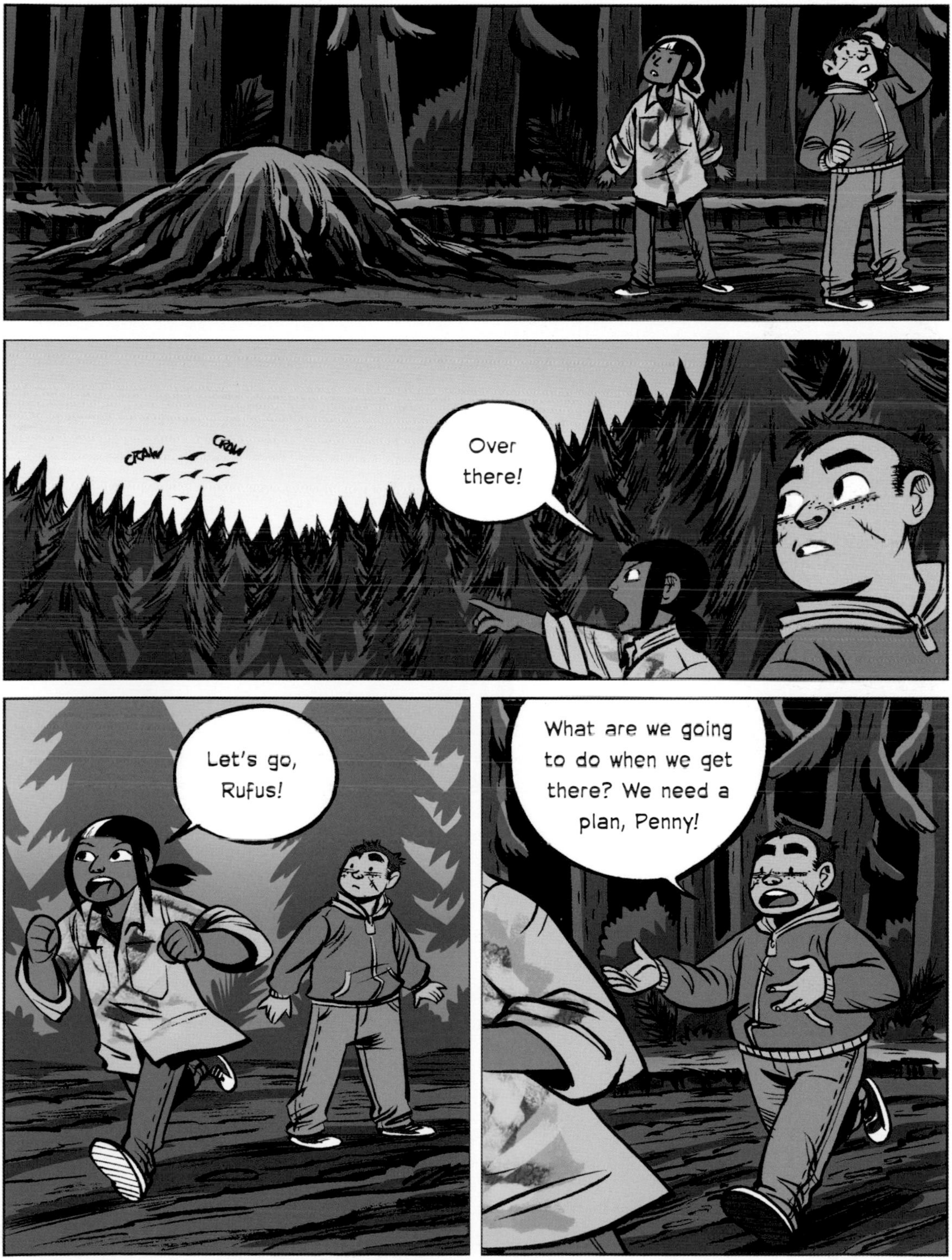
CRAW
CRAW
Over there!
Let's go, Rufus!
What are we going to do when we get there? We need a plan, Penny!

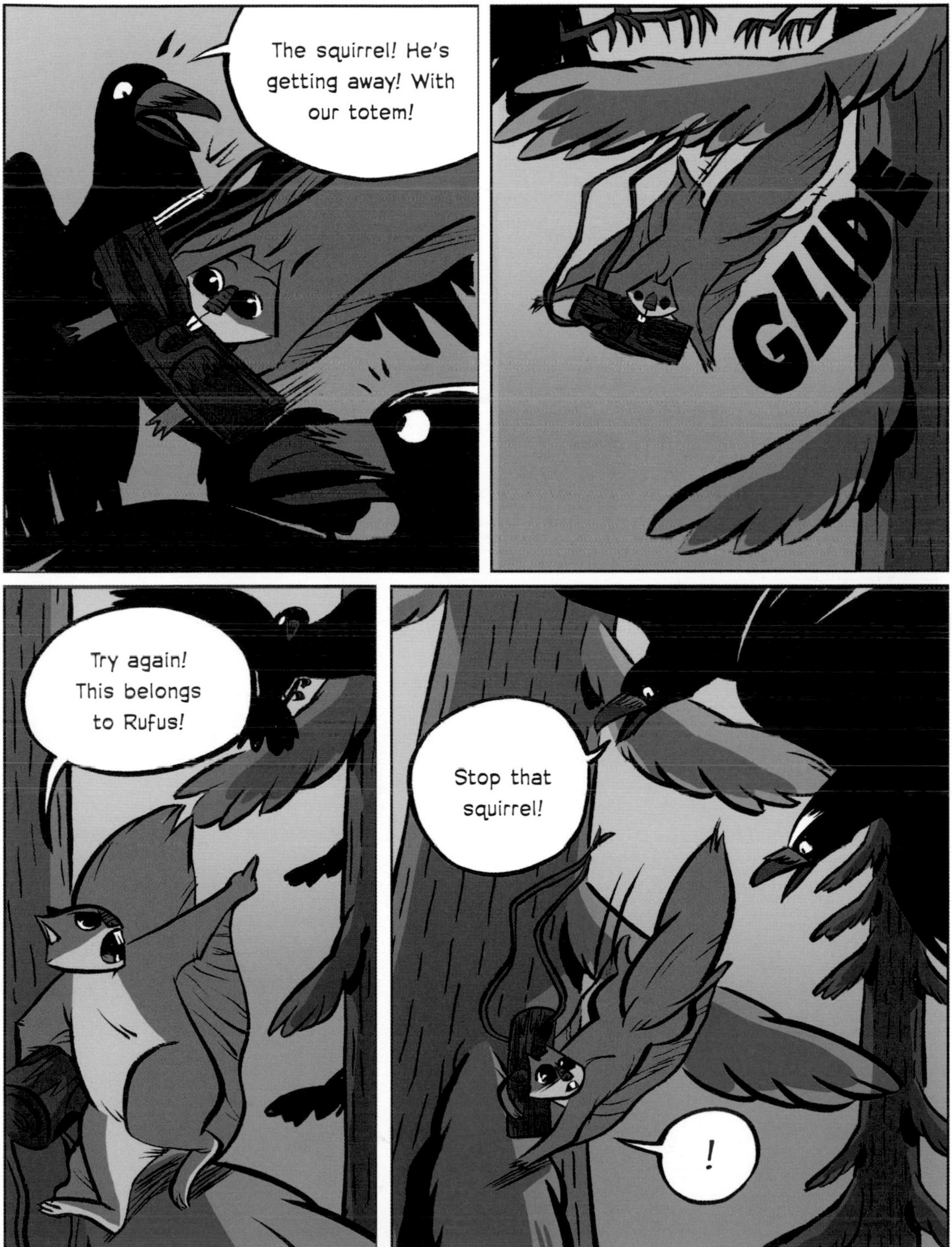
The squirrel! He's getting away! With our totem!
GLIDE
Try again! This belongs to Rufus!
Stop that squirrel!
!

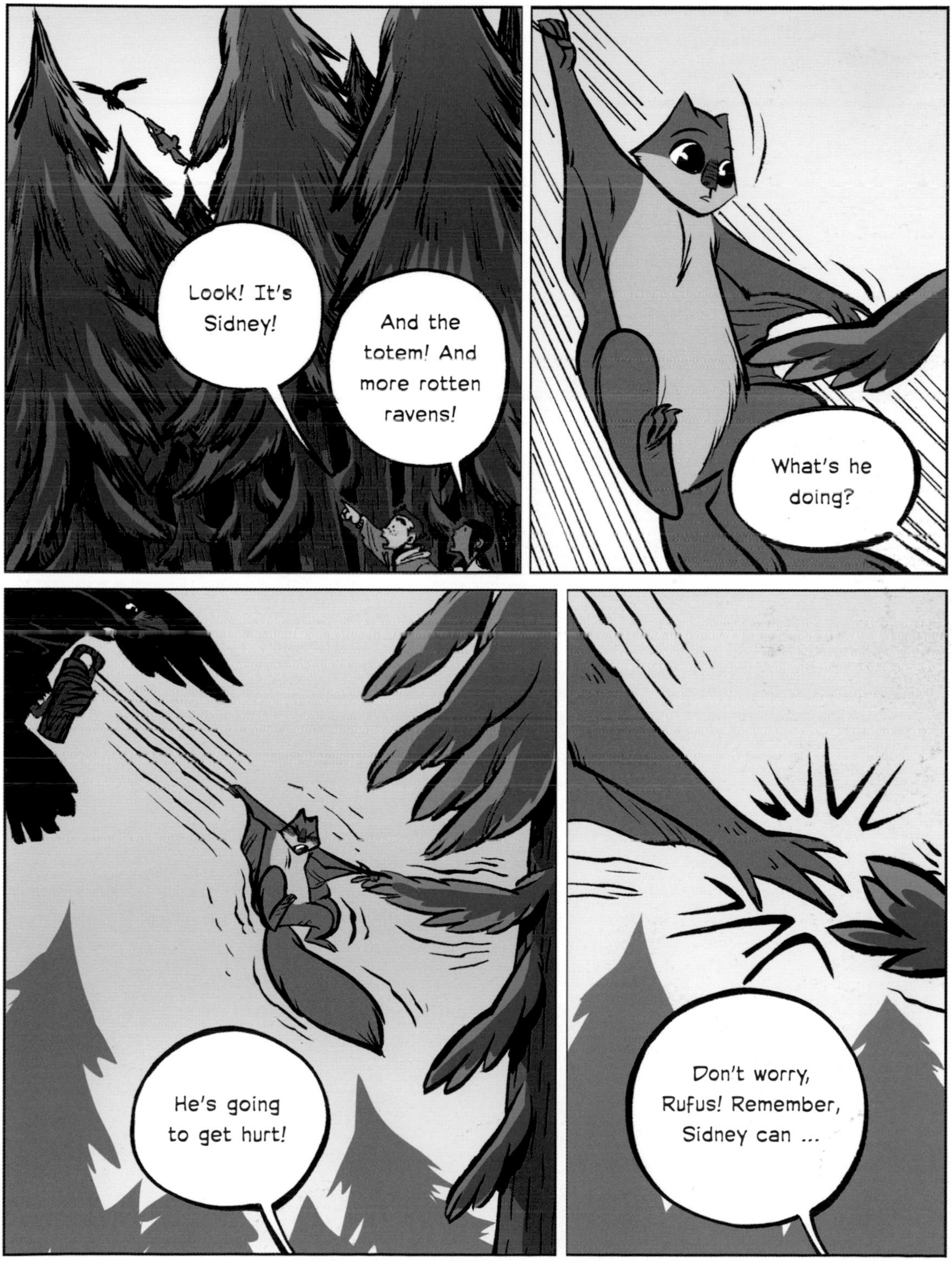
Look! It's Sidney!
And the totem! And more rotten ravens!
What's he doing?
He's going to get hurt!
Don't worry, Rufus! Remember, Sidney can ...

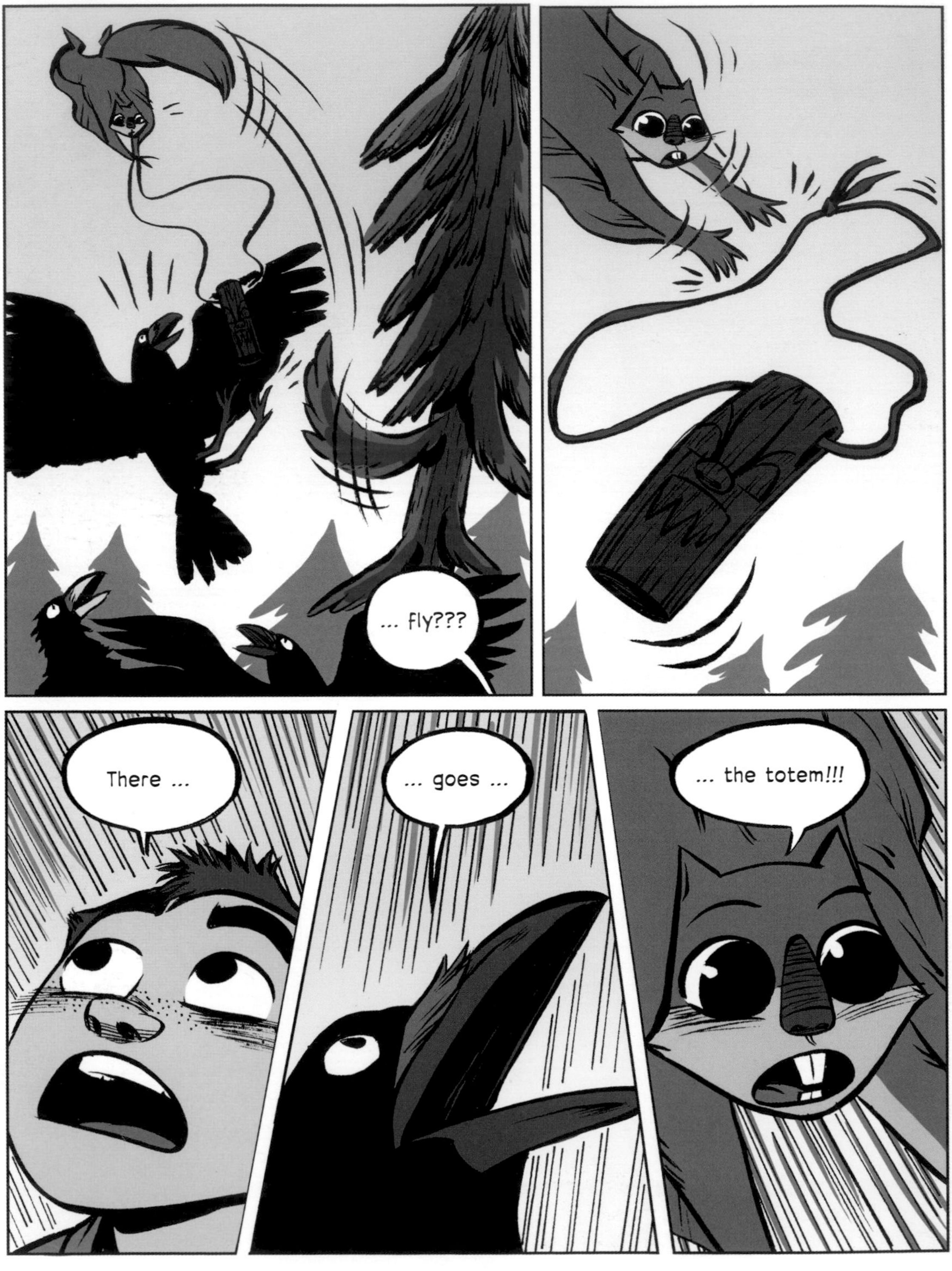
... fly???
There ...
... goes ...
... the totem!!!

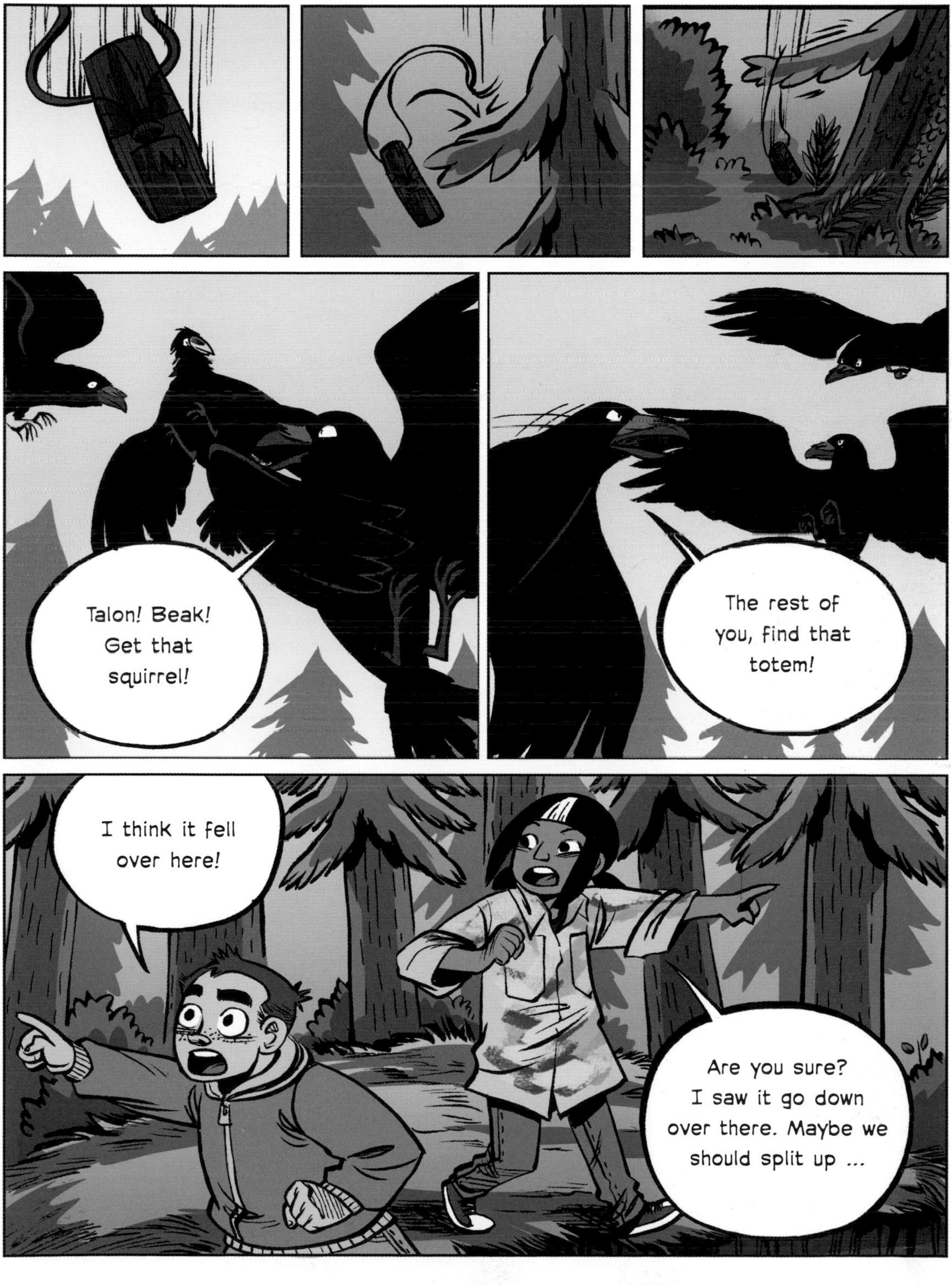
Talon! Beak! Get that squirrel!
The rest of you, find that totem!
I think it fell over here!
Are you sure? I saw it go down over there. Maybe we should split up ...

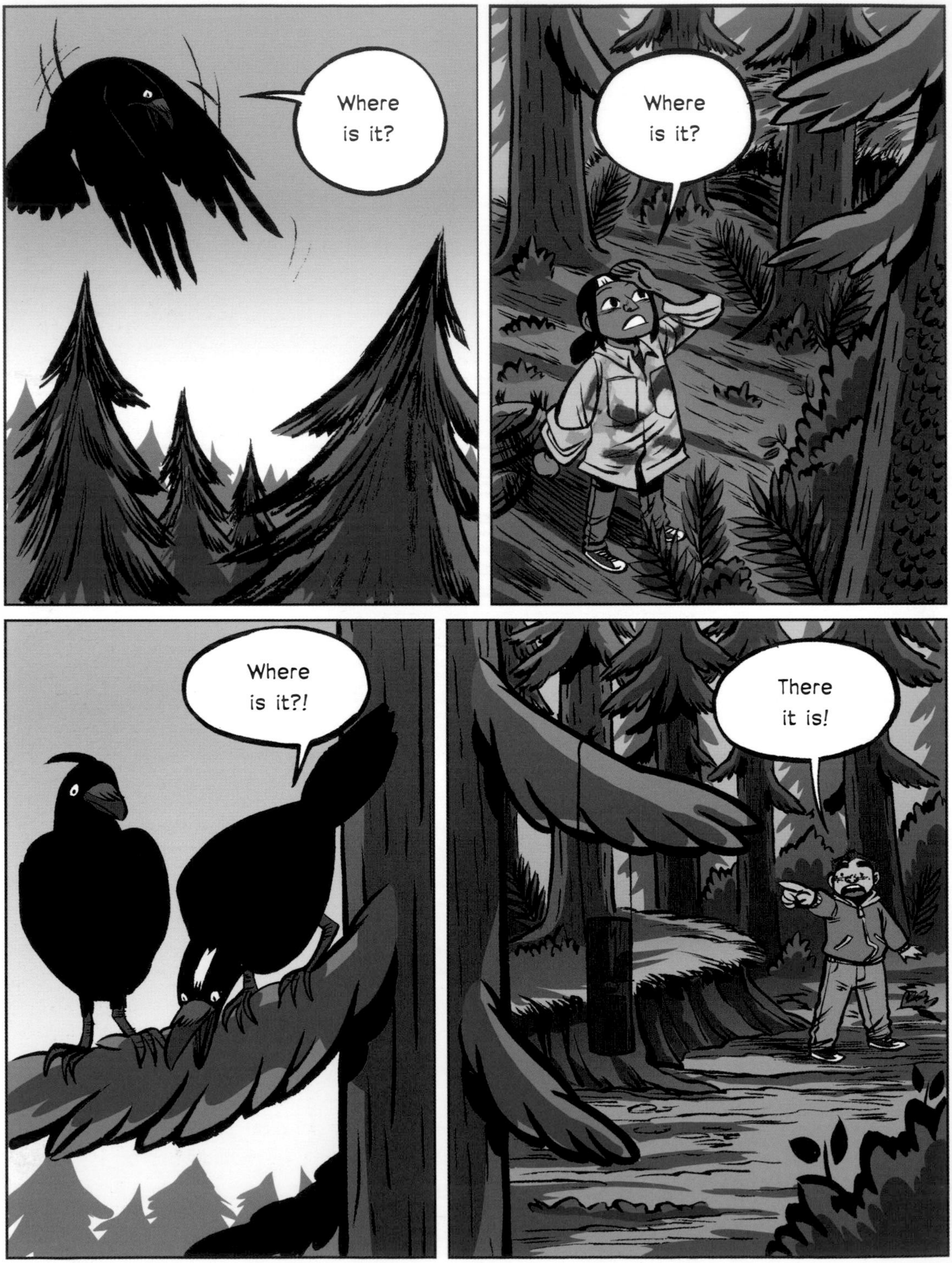
Where is it?
Where is it?
Where is it?!
There it is!

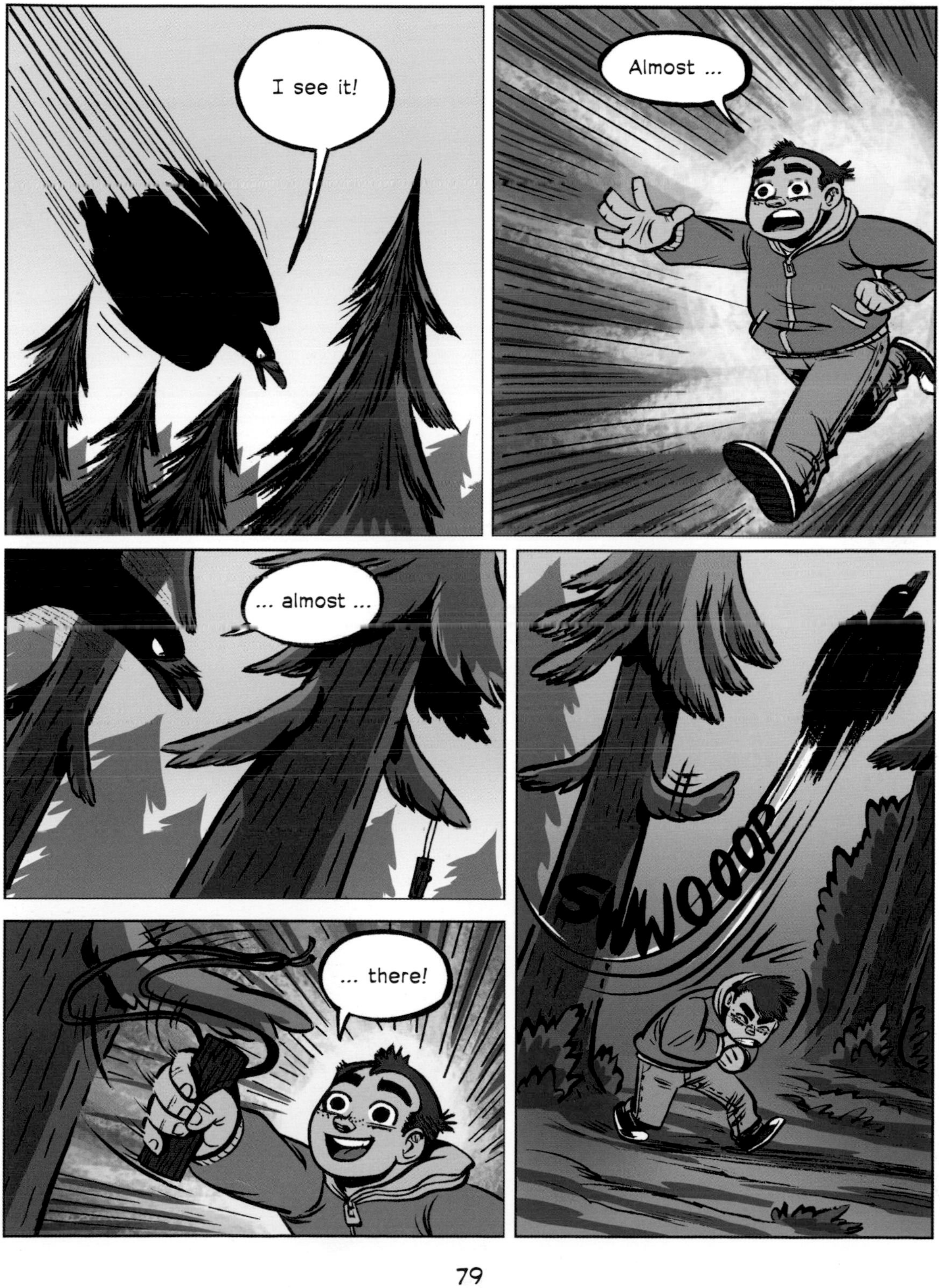
I see it!
Almost ...
... almost ...
... there!
SWOOOP

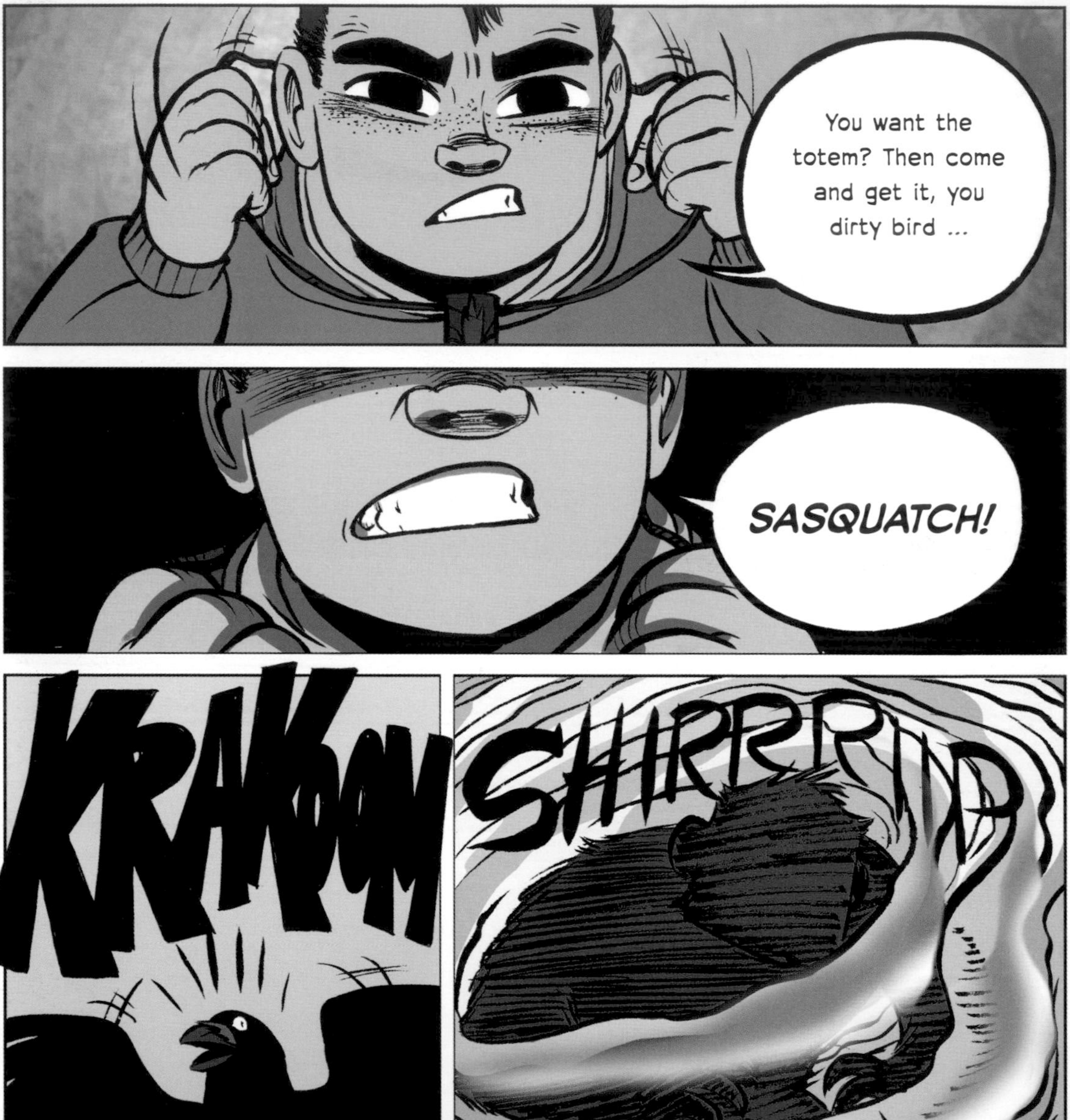
You want the totem? Then come and get it, you dirty bird ...
SASQUATCH!
KRAKOOM
SHIRRRRIIP
It's time to get ...

RRAAWESOME
Aw, man ... my clothes! Not rraawesome. Mom's going to kill me!

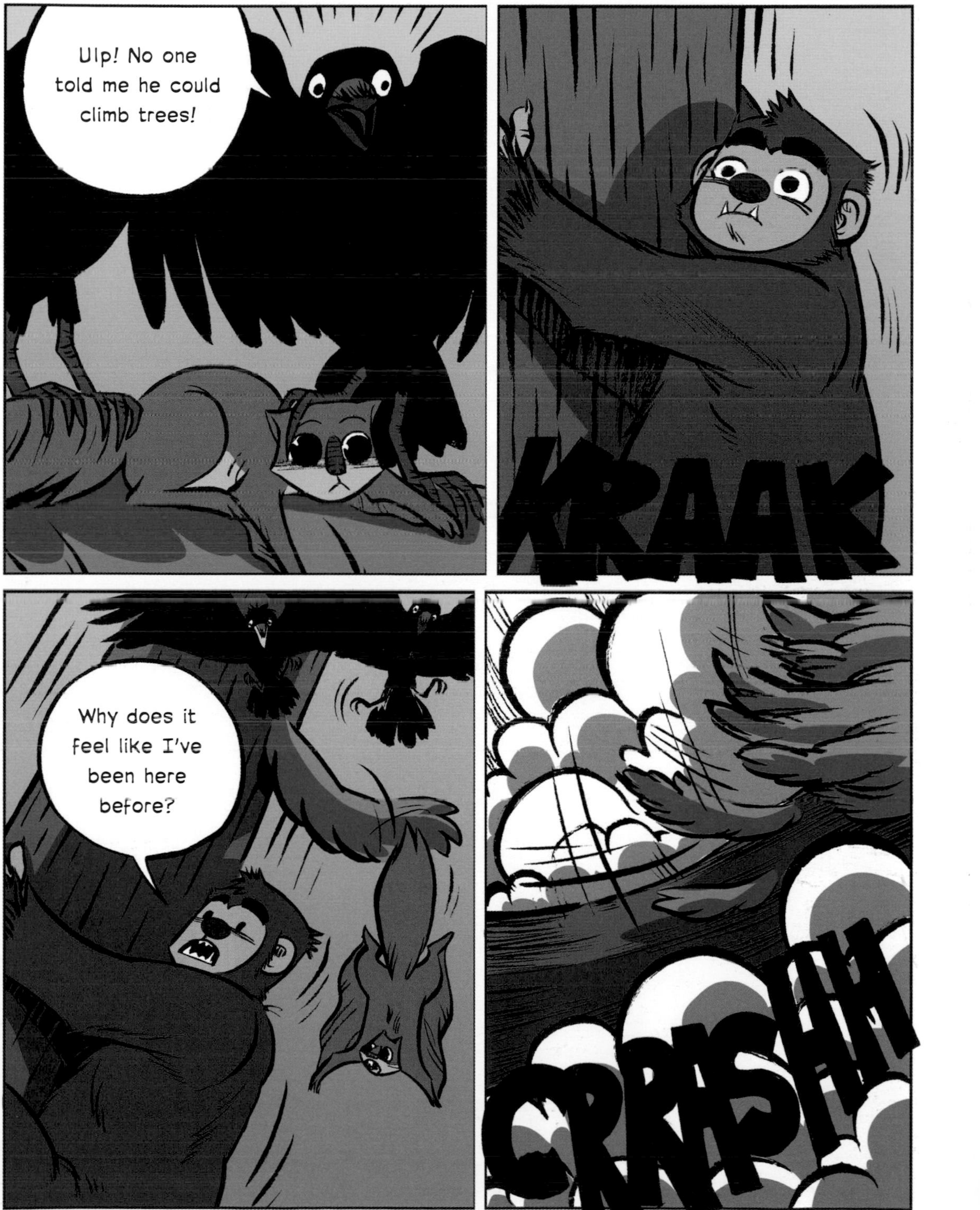
Ulp! No one told me he could climb trees!
KRAAK
Why does it feel like I've been here before?
CRRASHH

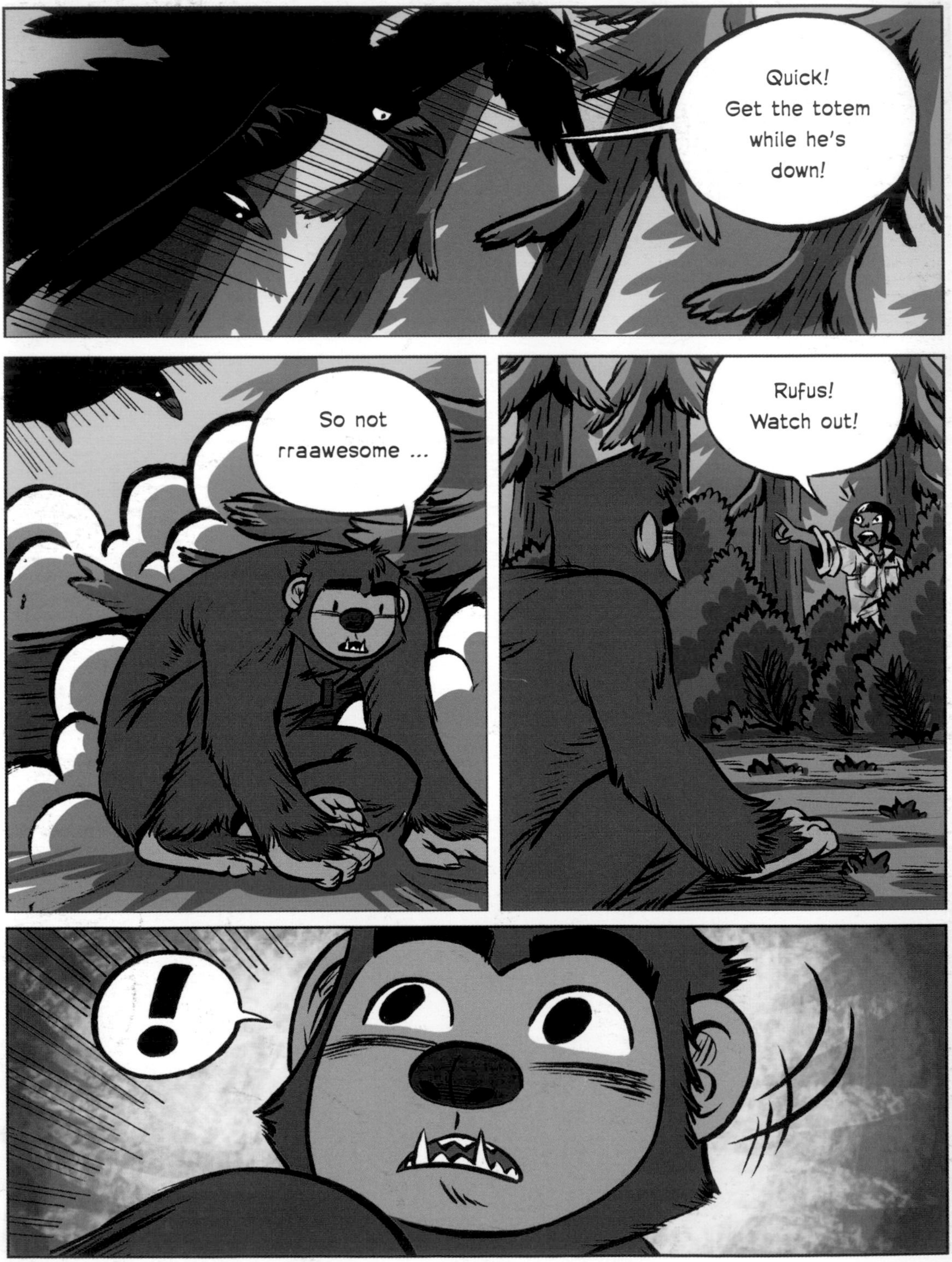

Quick! Get the totem while he's down!
So not rraawesome ...
Rufus! Watch out!
!

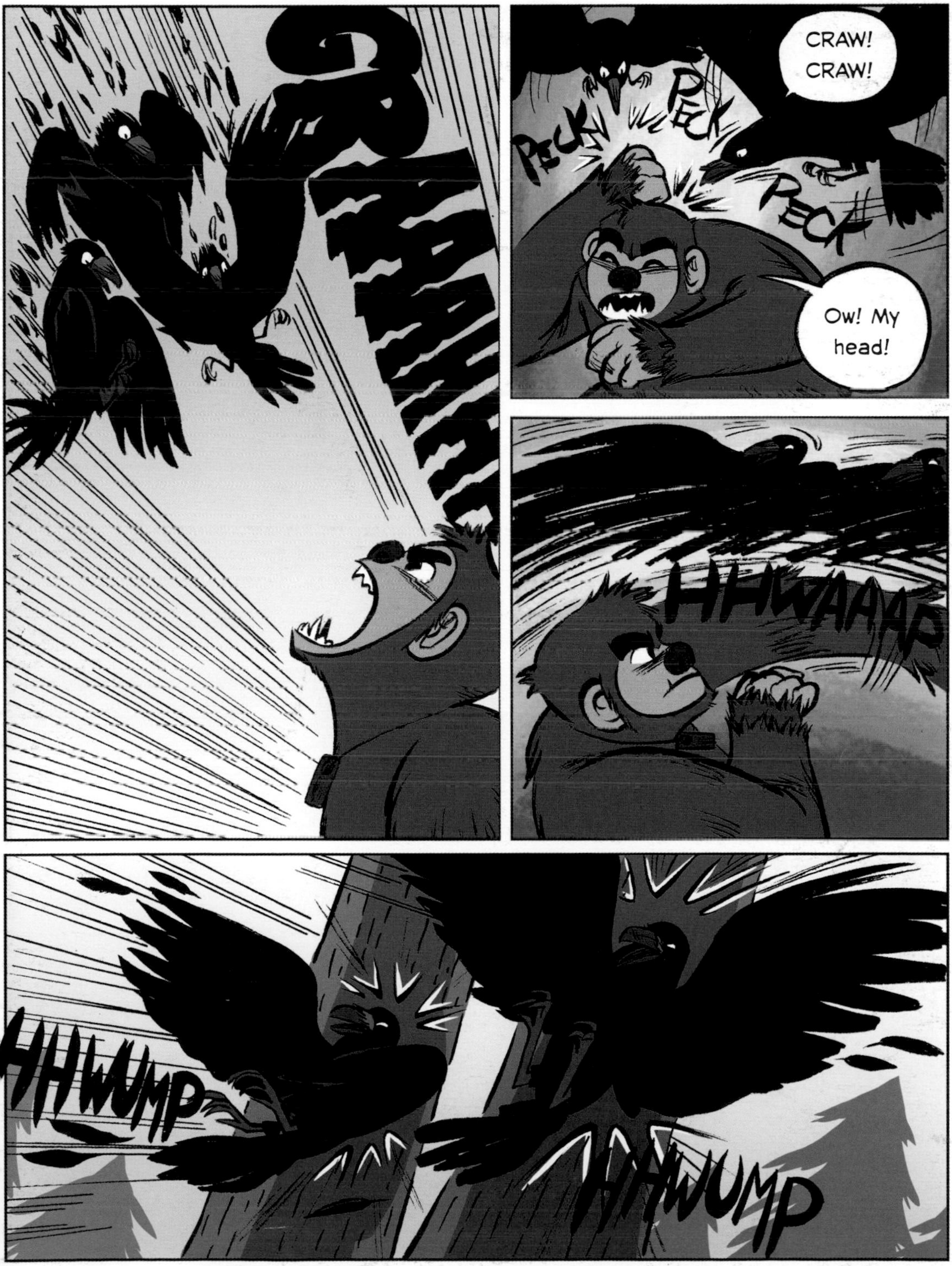
CRAW! CRAW!
PECK
PECK
PECK
Ow! My head!
HHWAAAP
HHWUMP
HHWUMP

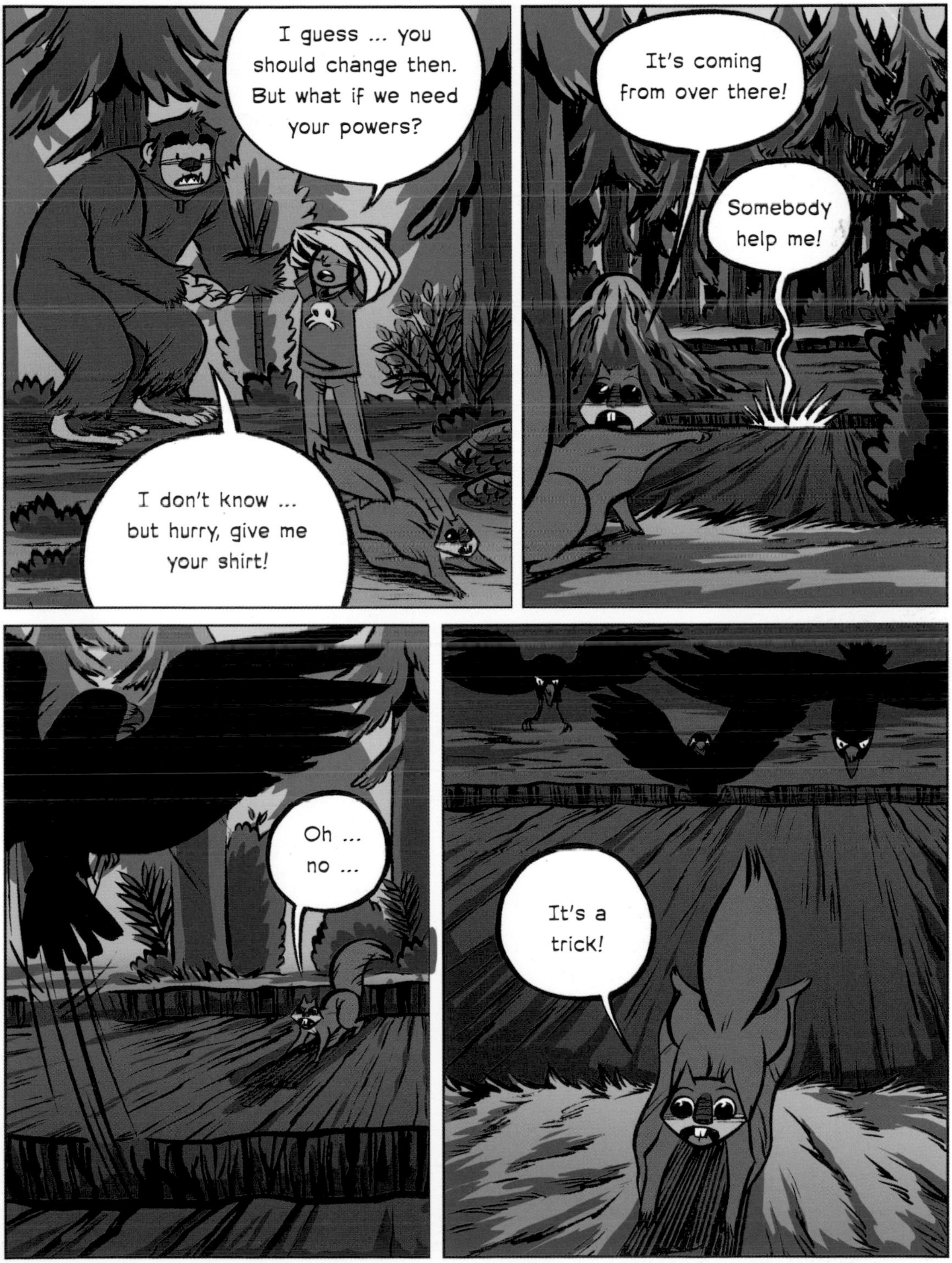
I guess ... you should change then. But what if we need your powers?
I don't know ... but hurry, give me your shirt!
It's coming from over there!
Somebody help me!
Oh ... no ...
It's a trick!

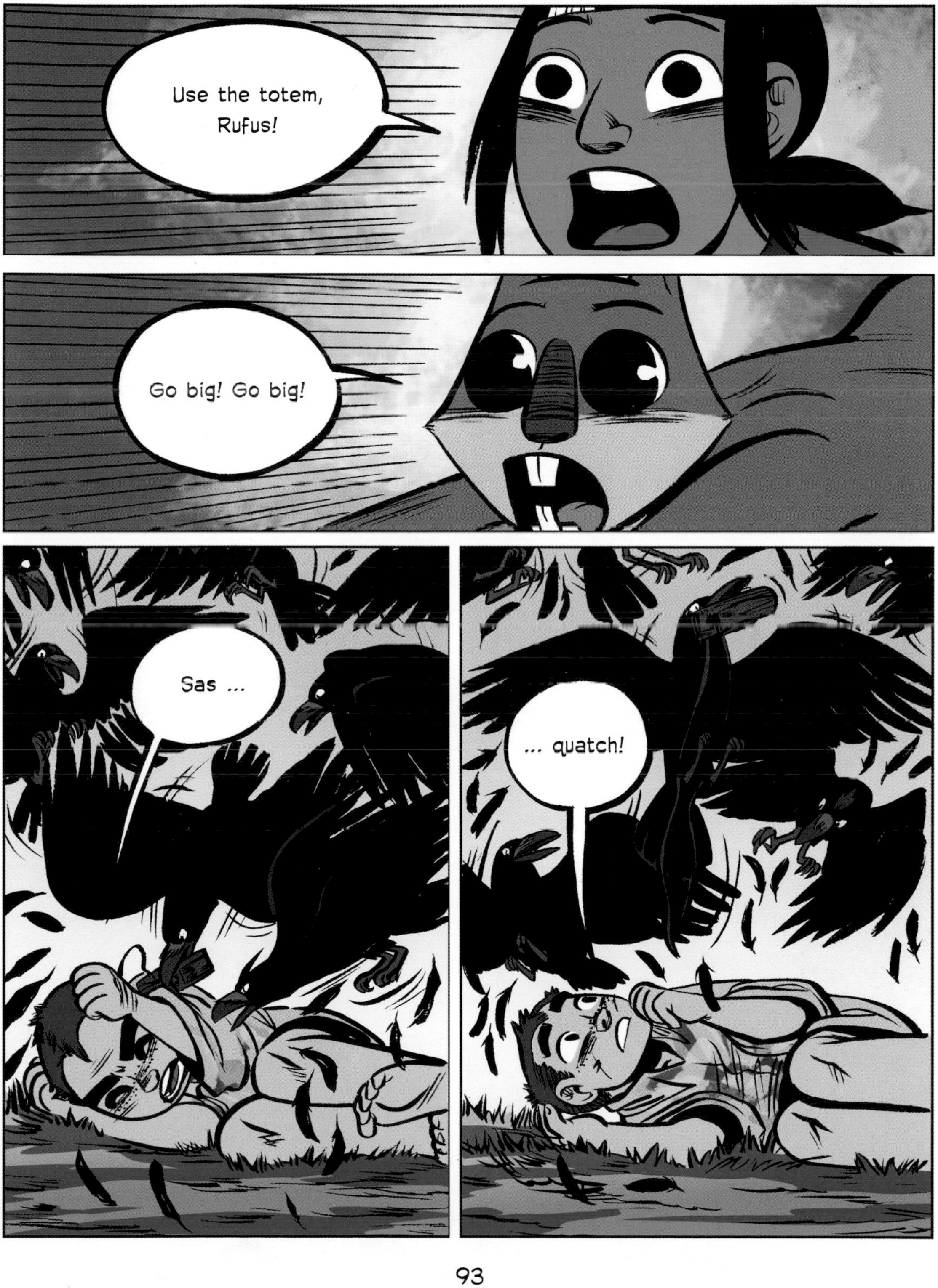

Use the totem, Rufus!
Go big! Go big!
Sas ...
... quatch!

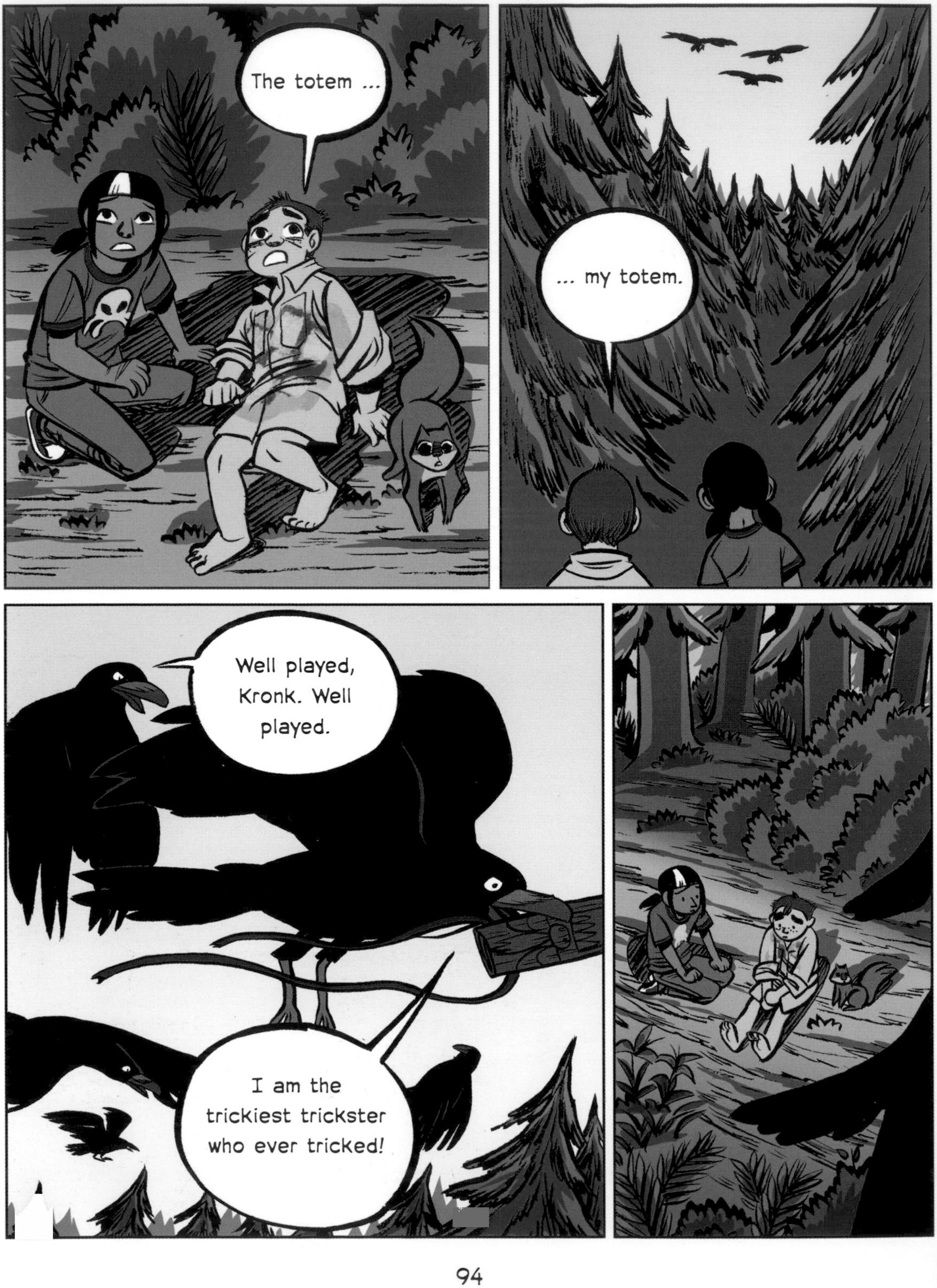
The totem ...
... my totem.
Well played, Kronk. Well played.
I am the trickiest trickster who ever tricked!

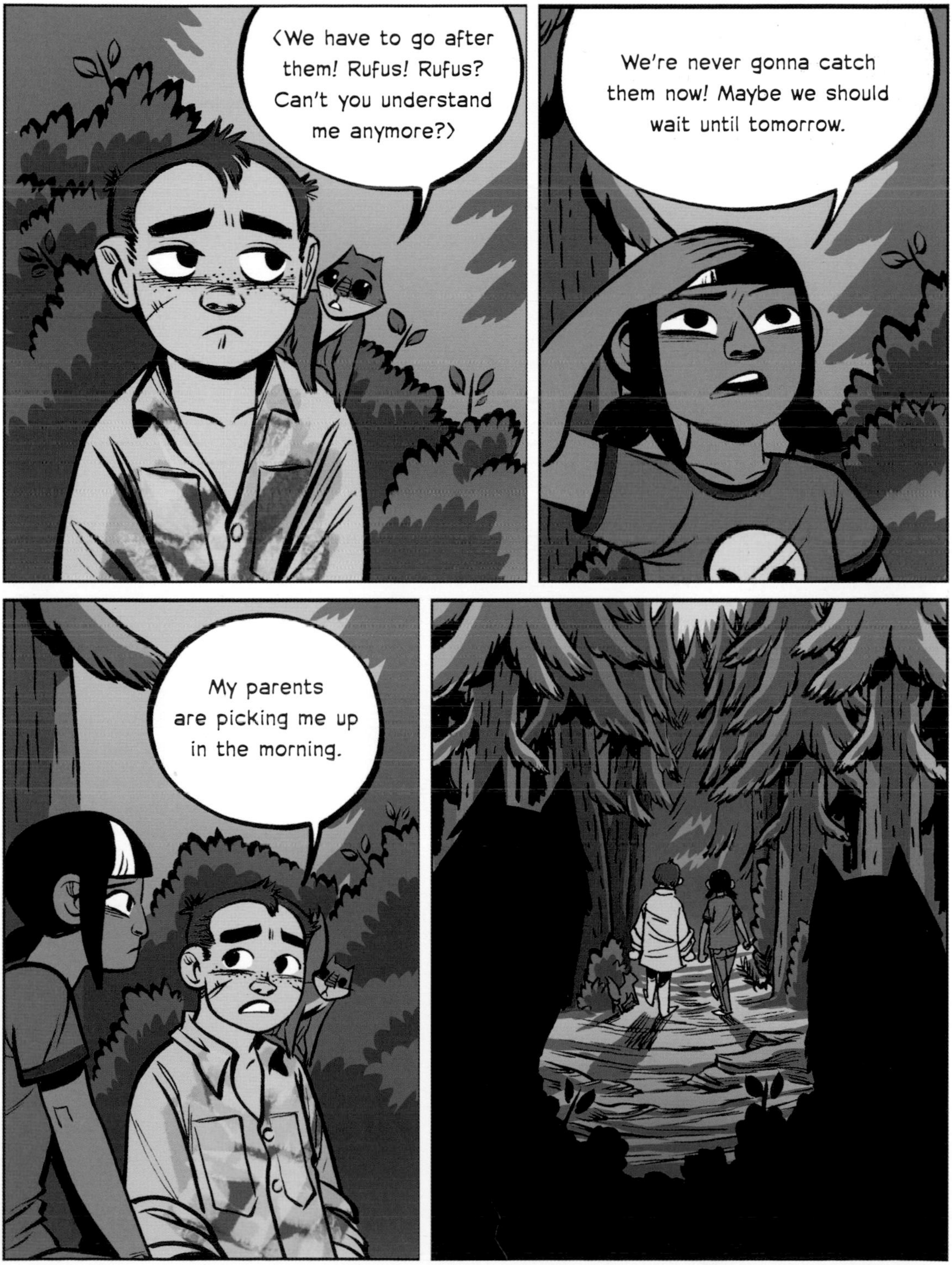

〈We have to go after them! Rufus! Rufus? Can't you understand me anymore?〉
We're never gonna catch them now! Maybe we should wait until tomorrow.
My parents are picking me up in the morning.

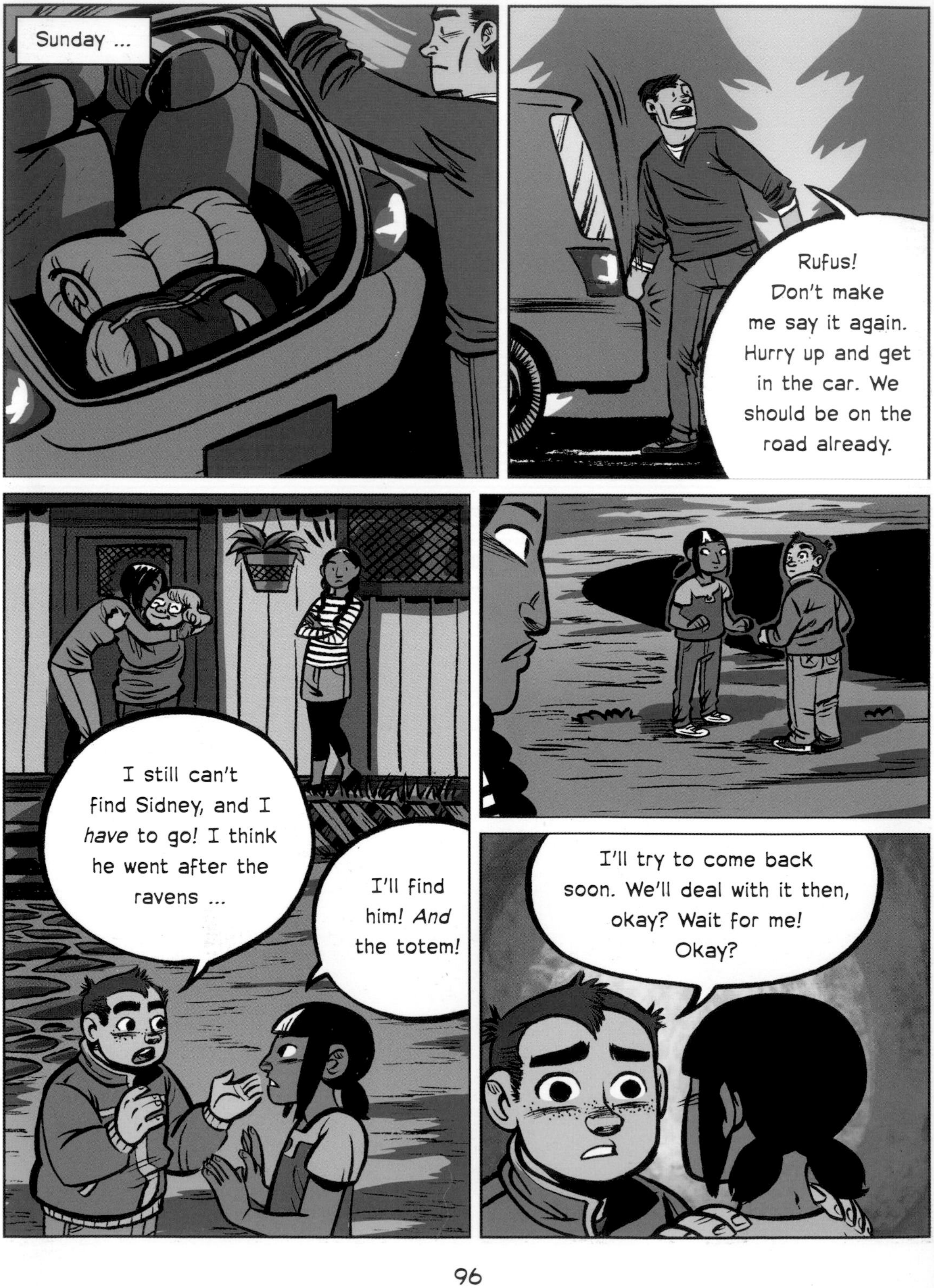
Sunday ...
Rufus! Don't make me say it again. Hurry up and get in the car. We should be on the road already.
I still can't find Sidney, and I *have* to go! I think he went after the ravens ...
I'll find him! *And* the totem!
I'll try to come back soon. We'll deal with it then, okay? Wait for me! Okay?

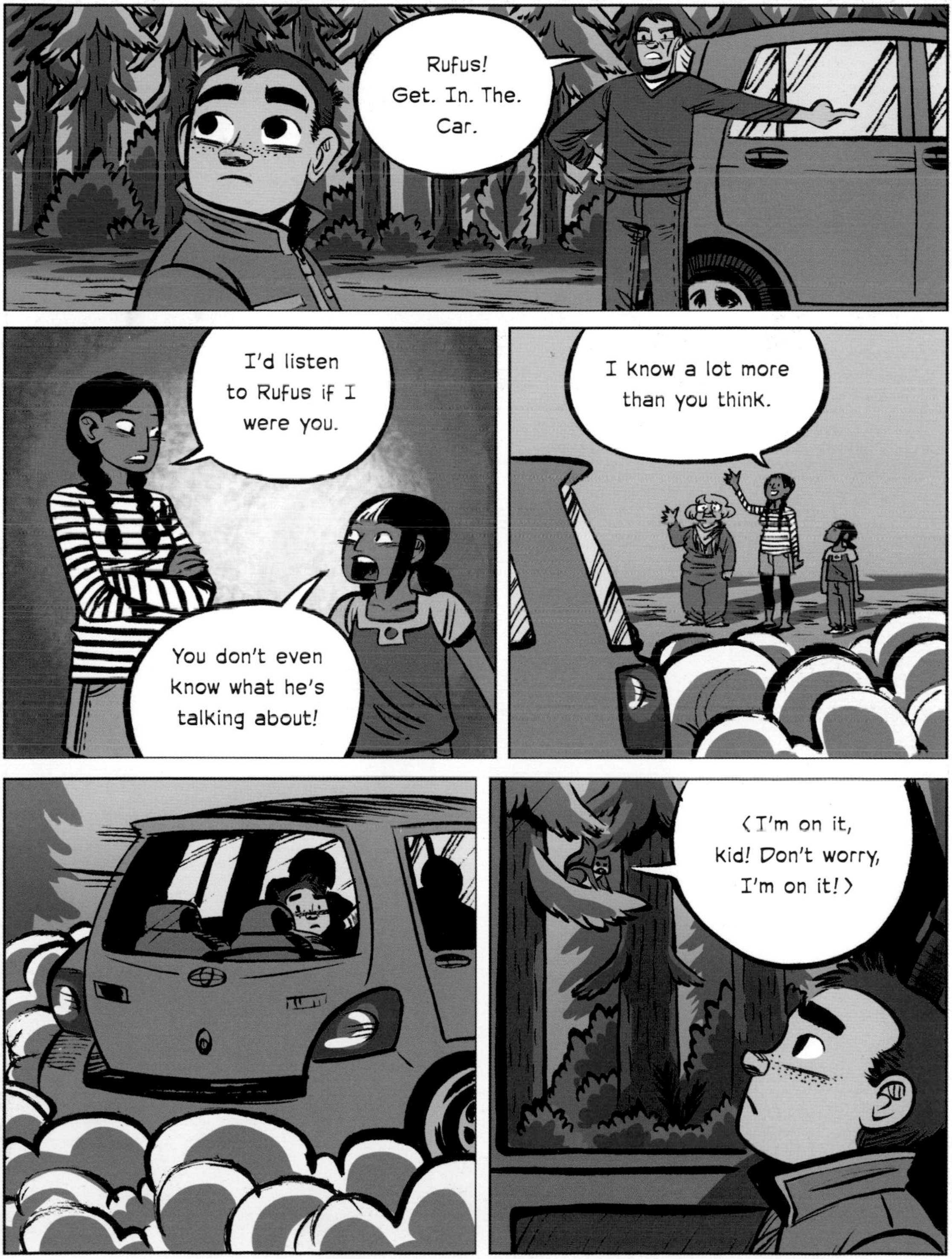
Rufus!
Get. In. The.
Car.
I'd listen
to Rufus if I
were you.
You don't even
know what he's
talking about!
I know a lot more
than you think.
‹I'm on it,
kid! Don't worry,
I'm on it!›

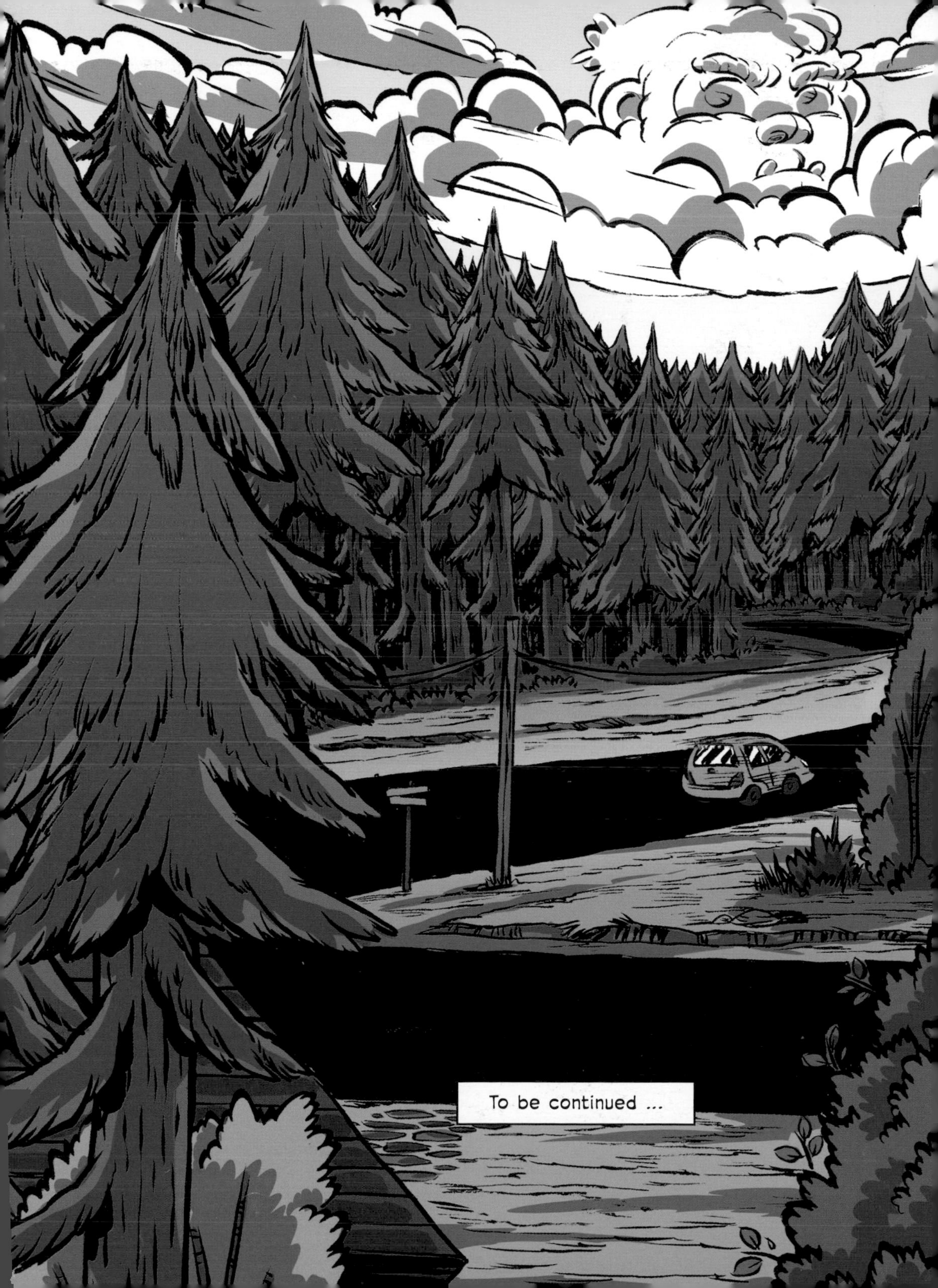
To be continued ...

DON'T MISS BOOK ONE IN THE BIGFOOT BOY SERIES

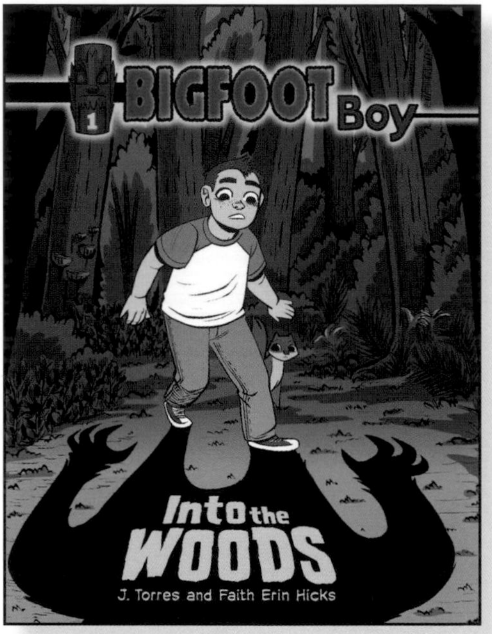
BIGFOOT Boy
1
Into the WOODS
J. Torres and Faith Erin Hicks

HC 978-1-55453-711-2
PB 978-1-55453-712-9

Praise for *Into the Woods*

★ "... magic, humor and just a hint of menace. ... This one gets everything just right. Be prepared for young Sasquatch fans roaring for more."

—*Kirkus Reviews,* starred review

"A solid introduction to a new adventure series, and young readers will clamor for a second volume."

—*Booklist*